Worse Things Than Spiders
And Other Stories

Worse Things Than Spiders
And Other Stories

By Samantha Lee

Shadow Publishing

WORSE THINGS THAN SPIDERS
AND OTHER STORIES

2nd Edition
This edition © Samantha Lee 2017
Cover artwork © Paul Bateman 2017

ISBN: 978-0-9539032-8-3

Shadow Publishing,
Apt 19 Awdry Court
15 St Nicolas Gardens
Kings Norton
Birmingham, B38 8BH, UK
david.sutton986@btinternet.com

This book is dedicated to

Alvaro Perez de Sevilla Guitard,
Marques de Cerro Vijil

Contents

ACKNOWLEDGEMENTS

Then to Dave Sutton, editor extraordinaire, who has used my
material in various outlets and on many occasions, allowing
these, and other stories, to find their place in the sun. To
Steve Jones, Neil Gaiman, Mike Ashley, Mary Danby,
Richard Davis and June Smith, for similar reasons.

And last but not least to my readers without whom, let's face it,
I'd be wasting my sweetness on the desert air
and simply talking to myself.

PREFACE

T O ME, WRITING a short story is a bit like having a baby. It begins with an orgasmic rush of excitement as the idea strikes. This is followed by a gestation period, internal details added or rejected in the safety of the creative womb. And finally, provided all has gone well and there have been no spontaneous abortions, we get to the painful part, the birth, when the fully formed foetal story struggles into the light of day.

Unlike writing a novel, with the plotting and planning and rigorous discipline of keeping all the balls in the air while getting the damn thing down on the page that that entails, short stories can be a form of light relief. But whatever their length, from the five minute sound bite to the nine thousand word novella, all of mine have followed this three pronged process. The only thing is that, like the animals in Orwell's farm, some have been 'more equal than others'.

There are tales that hit the page in ten minutes, while others have hung about for years, niggling in the pit of my stomach, until I gave them my full attention. Many have been stillborn. Practically none of them have lived up to that first ecstatic vision, losing something of their blithe spirit in the human translation.

But whatever, like children, once you've given them your best tender loving care, you needs must let them go out into the big wide world to fend for themselves. If they succeed you're delighted for them. If they fail you grieve on their behalf. But there's nothing more you can do for them. It's out of your hands. They have taken on a life of their own.

Here are a few of my offspring that made it past the first hurdle.

Be gentle with them.

Nice or nasty, they have their feelings too.

Samantha Lee
Malaga, November 2012

Of Spiders & Cats & Other Nasty Things
An Introduction to Samantha Lee
By David A. Sutton

I PUBLISHED SAMANTHA Lee's story 'Take Five' in issue 15 of *Fantasy Tales*, the small press magazine I edited with Stephen Jones from the seventies to the nineties. This story appeared in 1985 and we were quite taken with Sam's short, sharp horror tales and published 'Bon Appetite' a year later. And we've been fortunate enough to be able to use her stories in both *The Anthology of Fantasy & The Supernatural* and *Dark Terrors: The Gollancz Book of Horror*. These were fine introductions to Sam's horror yarns and it is with great pride that I am able to bring out this first collection of her spooky tales.

Sam doesn't sit in a grimy garret hiding away from the world while she pores over her computer, writing her latest genre work with feverish intent (of course it would be a nice, airy, sunny garret in Malaga, where she has mostly resided!). Well, perhaps she does, but her CV would seem to deride the clichéd notion of the writer hidden away from the world... Sam was born in Londonderry and studied at Newry Grammar School and later at London's Central School of Speech and Drama, then embarking on a career in light entertainment. She travelled the world for a decade and a half, singing (in six languages), before leaving show business to concentrate on her writing. As a performer she has done over 200 voice-overs for television and radio commercials, has hosted her own radio show on Talk Radio Marbella, co-hosted an evening slot on Central Radio, Benelmadena and been a guest on such diverse programmes as BBC Radio's *The Slice*, Northsound's *The Body Show*, Radio Clyde's *Sheila Duffy Presents* and the British Forces Network Radio Service in Gibraltar.

In 2008 her team "The Frankensteins" won both the jury and audience awards in the "24 hour challenge" at the Marbella International Film Festival, for their five minute short *Death Dancers*. Sam wrote the screenplay and played the villain, Mamma Sam, a loan-shark with an eye-patch and a bad attitude. Last year she was a jury member at Malaga University's "Fancine" Fantasy Film Festival chaired by Antonio Banderas.

In the early eighties she added another string to her bow, as a trainer and exercise consultant, running her Shape-up Studio in-house at the Aberdeen Petroleum Club for twelve years. Sam has been a guest lecturer on the QE2 and twice for Design Age at the Royal College of Art, at both the Aberdeen and Dundee Chambers of Commerce, the Aberdeen Breakfast Club, the Scottish Sport's Council, and for Age Concern. She was course tutor on relaxation techniques for Robert Gordon's University's Stress Management Courses, developer of "Lifeskills" Training Seminars and over the period 1991 - 1994 acted as Exercise Consultant, Trainer and Lecturer for the "Over 60's" exercise strand which she developed for the Aberdeen Health Board.

Her writing career spans literary criticism, poetry, self-development books, screenplays, articles, short stories and novels. Her work has been translated into French, Dutch, Spanish, Swedish, Italian, German, Croatian, Greek and Chinese... She has been a regular columnist for *Work-out Magazine* and for *The Marbella Times* and *Viva Espana*, with over two hundred articles published worldwide. Seventy-seven of her quirky short stories have featured on radio and television as well as in various best-selling anthologies and popular magazines. Her black comedy screenplay *The Gingerbread House* has been sold twice, first to Niagara Films and then to Random Harvest Productions.

Sam's short horror tales have been widely published, including in *The Pan Book of Horror Stories*, *Final Shadows*, the *Spectre* series and *Houses on the Borderland* among others. Of her sixteen full length books, the last five feature in Scholastic's best-selling "Point Horror" imprint. These are *Amy*, *The Bogle*, *The Belltower*, *Demon* and *Demon II*. Another in the series, *Demon III* was published last year exclusively on both Kindle and Smashwords ebooks. In fact most of her books are now out on Kindle, all of which have cover artwork by Dave Carson, who also designed the cover of this collection. One-off novels include *Childe Rolande* and *Dr. Jekyll and Mr. Hyde*. Her fantasy trilogy for younger readers, The Lightbringer series, *The Quest for the Sword of Infinity*, *The Land Where Serpents Rule*, *The Path Through the Circle of Time*, was published in the eighties.

In addition to her own writing, Sam has taught creative writing workshops in libraries and at literary Festivals all over Britain, particularly at London's Newham Library's Science Fiction Festival, "Out of this World". She acted as Master of Ceremonies at Fantasycon XI in 1986, writer in residence during the Year of Literature at the "Welcome to my Nightmare" weekend in Swansea and was a guest at *The Pan Book of Horror Stories* reunion at the 2010 World Horror Convention "Brighton Shock".

Now Sam can tell a story, be it heart-rending horror or charming jokey fantasies, such as 'Take Five', 'Scoop' or 'Jelly Roll Blues'. These will be a little light relief from the razor edged terrors in other yarns. She has a way of depicting torture and cruelty, often with a sharp eye on the humanitarian issues than underlie her themes. In 'The Island of the Seals' it is of course seal culling. In 'Nobody Thinks He's A Bad Guy' it's war crimes. These are dark stories indeed, told with just the right dollop of horror to thoroughly unnerve the reader. Then there are ghosts and mythical beings, the latter in 'Cat's Cradle', the former represented by the title story and 'Over My Dead Body'. Each of them unnerving in their own way. So here's the first ever volume of Sam's genre fiction – enjoy!

David A. Sutton
March 2013

WORSE THINGS THAN SPIDERS

T HE SPIDER CAME up through the knot in the floorboards, huge, hairy, bloated, scuttling sideways like a crab towards the bed. Jenny pulled the duvet up against her chin, shrugging herself back against the cheap quilting of the headboard, watching the monster progress across the threadbare carpet. She willed it to stop and it did. But only for a moment, pausing to observe her with a naked, malevolent stare, red eyes aglint, soft fat body perfectly suspended between cantilevered legs. A miracle of biological engineering. A Mexican stand-off.

I should get up, thought Jenny, and grab something and flatten it. Now. Before it's too late. But it was already too late. The spider seethed forward, launching itself at the end of the bed, surging up the leg, six inches across if it was a millimetre.

'Spiders don't bite.'

Her brother's scornful voice echoing down the years, as she'd stood in the bathroom, screaming herself blue in the face. Then her mother rushing in to flush the offending arachnid down the drain with the hairspray. The tips of its legs, like the ghost of dead fingers, holding on for grim death until the force of the water sluiced it, curled into a protective ball, down into the sewers, out into the open sea.

And that self-same brother slamming out, suitably indignant, yelling. 'It was only a spider. It wasn't going to hurt her. Murder, I call it,' while Jenny, shuddered her hysteria and her guilt into her mother's warm apron.

This spider emerged over the bed-head, come to get its own back on behalf of the species. The mother of all spiders, bent on revenge.

Fear galvanised Jenny into action. Reaching over to grab one of her Garfield slippers (a Christmas present from the aforementioned brother), she swiped frantically at the approaching creature. But horror of horrors, it began to swell, expanding like an inflating balloon, chameleon colour changing from black to bilious green to pus yellow, the whole putrid sack throbbing with bright scarlet eyes.

Jenny flailed the air, but the spider, big as a rat now, easily avoided her blows, feinting to right and left as it zigzagged past her knees and thighs and up over her stomach heading towards her jugular vein. She opened her mouth to scream but the sound came out like a bell, a telephone bell, catapulting her out of the nightmare into the cold grey light of the January morning.

'Jenny? I was just about to hang up.' It was her agent.

'Hello Lois,' she tried not to sound too eager. 'Sorry. I was asleep.'

'At this hour? Lucky for some. Anyway dear, I've got a job for you.'

'A job?' Visions of glossy commercials swam in Jenny's imagination, a West End run, a TV play, maybe even a small part in a feature film? 'What sort of a job?'

'A role playing job.'

Jenny's heart sank. 'Oh,' she said.

'Don't sound so disappointed dear, it's good money. A hundred a day for two days AND expenses AND three meals a day at the hotel. What was the last time you worked?'

'November,' mumbled Jenny. If she hadn't temped at Selfridges during the Christmas rush, she'd be out on the streets by now.

'Precisely. Beggars can't be choosers, dear.'

'I know. I'm sorry. I didn't mean to sound ungrateful.'

'That's all right. Don't despair. The first year out of Drama School is always the worst. Things'll pick up as your face becomes more familiar. You're a pretty girl, talented, that red hair is quite unique. If it's any consolation, these things take time.'

Jenny said nothing. What was there to say? A money spider crawled up the phone flex. She whacked it frantically with the Yellow Pages, cringing as the matter splattered on the cover.

'Meanwhile, this is a nice little bread and butter job. More and more firms are doing these training courses. Putting their executives into unaccustomed situations and seeing how they shape up. Lucky for us they need professional actors to play them off against. Do you have a skirt?'

'A skirt?'

'A sensible skirt, dear. Nothing outré. And a pair of low-heeled shoes and a white blouse. You're playing a room-service maid. Nine sharp, day after tomorrow. Take a taxi to the Horden Hotel. The company will pay...'

Excerpt from the North London Chronicle. January 5th, 1846.

GRISLY FIND AT HAMPSTEAD HOME.

Staff from the Auctioneering Firm of Mangold and Reece, clearing out the effects of Mr Ezekial Horden in the event of that gentleman's death from heart failure, were horrified to find human remains in the attic room of the large mansion house. The skeleton, which experts believe to have been there for at least ten years, appears to be that of a young child, whose malformed limbs would, in life, have give it the appearance of a human spider. The late Mr Horden's wife, formerly actress Sarah Sotherby, died some twelve years ago. A report has been sent to the Office of Public Prosecutions.

Seven of them at the briefing. Seated at a round table, warmly adjacent to a roaring log fire, filling their faces with coffee and croissants, while outside the snow fell heavy on the hills and dales of Hampstead Heath.

Three "management". Marjorie Jewell, whizz-kid psychologist, already pulling in forty k a year. Norman Parker, (Marjorie's Mentor), manner smooth as his balding pate, Sociologist and Devisor of "The Course". And Simon Mallow, Head of Personnel at Amogen Oil, on hand to see the Company got its money's worth.

Four "actors". Jim Bolton, a "face", familiar of the box but to whom no-one could ever give a name. Diane de Montfort, an ageing ingénue still hoping for the big break. David Dashwood, immaculately camp in sharp suit and sharper tongue. And Jenny.

'There are twelve "players",' Norman explained, 'and the Course is designed to teach them Management skills.'

'People management,' Marjorie interjected. 'As opposed to Business management.'

'Just as well,' said Simon, full of his own importance. 'Most of these blokes are Managers already. But they've come up from the shop floor. No finesse. My way or the highway approach. Doesn't go down too well with the workforce nowadays.'

The actors nodded sagely.

'The Course,' Norman went on, not best pleased at having his "schpeel" interrupted, 'has been designed to teach these men to influence their employees' thinking.'

'Manipulate them, you mean?' said Jenny.

Marjorie raised one of her perfectly plucked eyebrows and smiled patronisingly.

'*Not* a word we'd use, "manipulate". Smacks of Goebbels. Influencing sounds more...civilised. We're in the business of persuasion rather than possession.'

Cold. So cold. Snow on the slates above the slope of the ceiling. Icy wind cutting through the crack in the pane that broke the day they took Mama away. Banging on the window for her to take me too. Don't leave me behind. Please Mama. Please. All that warm red hair, shut in that cold black box, sunk in the cold black earth. Why did you leave me Mama? Especially with him. Dear Mama. So loving before he came. Your warm arms around me, your sweet voice singing me to sleep. He says I'm an abomination. Cold. And lonely. No-one to visit. No-one to care with Mama gone. Cold and hungry. And so weak. Too weak even to get to the window. To watch the snowflakes through the bars, falling like feathers from a burst pillow onto the cobbles of the courtyard. Just to see an occasional groom hurrying through with a bucket of warm mash or a blanket maybe for the horses. To call down and get a wave, a grin. Only a dream. No more horses. No more Mama. So weak. So tired. So cold.

They put Jenny in the attic room for the sake of authenticity. She was only an upstairs maid, after all. All morning the actors had spent talking themselves into character, re-acting and interacting until their new egos began to take precedent.

The proper work would start tomorrow when the course candidates, fired by a day of lectures, would try out their "influencing skills". Instead of working for an oil company, they were to pretend to be consultants to a Leisure Group, which had just bought a run-down family hotel. By interviewing the actors (who in their turn represented the Hotel Management) they had to deduce what was wrong with the running of the place and find ways of turning it into a going concern.

Each actor was given an office in which to see the consultants. Except for Jenny who, as the lowliest member of the hierarchy, had been designated a hovel which would, in all probability, have really been her bedroom, if she had really been an upstairs live-in maid. She hated the room. She hated the set-up. She hated the part. Because Jenny, the actress, was slowly becoming Jenny, the live-in maid, ill-educated, unappreciated, but with a burning ambition to "better herself".

She laid her script down and moved to the old-fashioned sash window. The room was stuffy and damp at the same time. Stifled, she reached her hand between the bars, to try to let in some air, then pulled away with a shriek as a massive spider unravelled itself from a dust-ball.

Why bars? she thought, retreating towards the bed, away from the spider which skittered unhindered, over the windowsill, down the wall and across to the far end of the room where the eaves sank into a shadowed corner.

Across the courtyard, where the wisps of mist rose from the car pool to hang like wraiths in the gathering dusk, lights were coming on in the hotel dining room. Groups of men in expense account suits, filtered in to deploy themselves round pink linen tablecloths.

A sense of dread descended on the two Jennies—the actress, imprisoned in this small dank room with her pre-show nerves—and the upstairs maid, shut away from her "betters" —out of sight out of mind. A sudden, horrible feeling of being watched overcame her. Stop it. Get a grip. You're just imagining things. She craned her head, wanting, yet not wanting to see into the dim corner, where now the spider lurked. She would have to get rid of it before she went to bed. The thought of it crawling over her in the dead of night didn't bear thinking about.

Came a shadowy movement as something gathered itself together and hobbled out into the light. Body crouched between twisted limbs, matted hair falling in great tangles around the sunken eyes. Slowly, it held out manacled claws towards her. Slowly, the slack mouth formed a single word...'Mama'.

Jenny burst into the dining room, hair flying, eyes popping, screaming at the top of her voice. Norman Parker, summoned by the Head Waiter, hustled her out into the foyer and shook her till her brains rattled.

'What on earth is going on?' he said, through clenched teeth. 'You were supposed to stay in your room.' But this statement only brought a fresh burst of wailing as Jenny swung her head from side to side, hiccoughing and snorting.

Parker thrust her at Marjorie, who held the girl at arm's length in case the tears coursing down her face should mark the silk suit which had cost her an arm and a leg. 'See if you can do something with her.'

'Me?'

'Yes, you. You're the psychologist. You're the woman. Stop posing for once and do your job. That's what I pay you for.'

'She says there's something in the room,' said Marjorie, emerging from the Ladies some minutes later. 'But that's all I can get out of her. She seems to be in a state of shock.'

'Get her out here,' said Simon Mallow, grimly. 'I've got her agent on the phone. Let's see if she can talk some sense into her.

So Jenny was marched, shamefaced and still shaking, out to the very public phone to be confronted by an irate Lois wanting to know whether she had gone stark, staring bonkers?

'I can't go back into that room Lois, please don't make me,' wailed Jenny, trying her best to sound rational. 'There's something in there, something horrible... a sort of spider thing.'

Lois sighed. 'I know all about the spiders, Jenny, about your brother's pet tarantula that escaped and got into your bed. A bad experience. But you can't let this phobia rule your life.'

'No, no, it wasn't an ordinary spider it was... much bigger... like a... like a...' she stopped, at a loss to describe what it was she'd seen under the eaves.

'Now you listen to me, Jenny Carter,' said Lois sharply. 'I stuck my neck out to get you this job. They wanted someone with more experience but I personally recommended you.'

Jenny looked up at the sea of unsympathetic faces as Lois ranted on, telling her she was making a spectacle of herself, telling her she was letting everybody down, telling her that if she didn't get right up to that room this instant, she would not only be looking for another job, she'd be looking for another agent, and Lois would personally see to it that she never worked in "the business" again.

Mama running. No, not Mama. The door slamming. Silence. Don't leave me. Please, don't leave me alone again. Can I get to the window? Chains sore on my ankle. If he doesn't feed me soon my thin bones will slip through. Free then, like the sparrows on the windowsill, leaving star-shapes in snow with their hop, hop, hop. Flying away into the leaden sky, as I would like to fly, out of this awful place. Fly to where Mama lies under the frozen ground, creep into her arms and feel her stroke my hair and soothe me asleep and blot out the pain and the loneliness and this terrible never-ending cold.

Jenny stood stock still for at least a minute after Marjorie left, overcome by the enormity of having to spend the night in such a place. Soft sounds of jangling cutlery, people chatting, the world going on as usual, seeped through the bedroom door. While inside an alternative universe bubbled and frothed, bulging with unknown terrors, out of which at any moment, the bogey-man might jump to bite off her head.

Jenny collapsed onto the bed, knees drawn up to her chest, hugging herself tight to steady her jangled nerves, closing her eyes against the darkness in the corner. Don't look, she told herself. Don't look. There's nothing there, while aloud she said...

'I need this job. I need this job.'

Foetal, semi-comatose, she listened to the sound of her own heart while about her the air thickened with menace and the hairs on the back of her hands grew rigid as Dr. Jekyll's in anticipation of an emerging Mr. Hyde.

And then another sound began to punctuate the pounding of her own heart's beat. A sound fit to freeze the blood. The unmistakeable sound of an abandoned child, crying quietly to itself.

Jenny lay for a moment absorbing the sound. Then she sat up. The light from the winter moon, spilling into the room, threw a pattern of elongated bars across the carpet, pointing to the dark spot under the eaves.

What am I afraid of, thought Jenny, surely not of this?

Wrapping her courage around her, she moved across to the darkness, to the dark thing crouched in it, huddling under the wall's curve, curled as the spider had curled itself against the finality of the drain, rocking its poor bent body and weeping as though its heart would break. And Jenny did what any normal human being would do. She knelt down and took the child in her arms, felt its small insubstantial body turn in against her, rocked it as mothers have rocked their offspring since time immemorial, feeling it snuggle into her as she stroked the matted hair, speaking words of comfort as it moved closer still, melting inside her until her arms were empty and her body suddenly full of pain. The red-hot pain of festering sores, the throbbing pain of disease-stiffened joints, the cold, gnawing pain of terminal hunger. But worse than any of this, the pain in the centre. Ache of loss and absolute abandonment. Total desolation sweeping through her, burning like fire. Worse pain that Jenny had ever known. More than she could cope with. More than she could stand.

MAGGIE. Stark out, she was, flat on the floor. Stiff as a board. Well. You can imagine what I thought?

TRACE. Another one bites the dust?

MAGGIE. Too true. After that last bloke, I never thought they'd put another client in there.

TRACE. So what did you do?

MAGGIE. Put the tray down, didn't I? Nice bit of chicken, avocado and prawns, fruit salad.

TRACE. Better than they feed us.

MAGGIE. Say that again. Anyway, she was coming round by then, moaning a bit, moving her hands and feet, you know, like a dog does when it's having nightmares. So I sloshed some wine down her throat and she sat up, right as rain. Ate the dinner like she hadn't seen food in a month.

TRACE. You never! What did she say about... you know... passing out?

MAGGIE. Said she'd had a dizzy spell, time of the month and that. Asked me not to tell. Said she didn't want the management thinking she was neurotic.

TRACE. No mention of seeing anything?

MAGGIE. Not a dickie-bird. Asked if I had a sleeping pill? Said she wanted to make sure she got a decent night's kip.

TRACE. (shuddering). In that room? Rather her than me.

Jenny waited until the chambermaid had gone, until the Hotel sounds had dimmed away into the silence. Then, wrapping up warm in winter coat and boots, she let herself out of the hated room, and stole downstairs, across the empty courtyard, through the main body of the slumbering building, past the night porter snoring lightly at his post and out into the midwinter night.

Inside her, the child slept, rising and falling with her heartbeat, warm for the first time in several lifetimes. Jenny hummed quietly to it as she trudged through the snow, a four-note phrase remembered from her own childhood. She had no notion where she was going, moving instinctively for over an hour, feet following one after another until she came to the cemetery, where the lock opened as if by magic, and the great gates creaked back without so much as an "open sesame".

She was tired now, feet flagging on the icy gravel, the moon high, Karl Marx's moustache jaunty with dangling icicles. She stumbled on between the rimed gravestones, brushing snow off inscriptions, finding at last the one she sought... a face, not unlike her own, superimposed on a theatrical angel, crowned with wild, Pre-Raphaelite hair.

Gratefully, she sank to her knees and her voice came out clear and sharp as frost, hanging in a cloud on the listening air.

'Georgie' she said, patting her stomach. 'Wake up. We're home.'

It was a Mrs. Ethel Barnes, paying a visit to her long defunct husband Raymond, who found her, stiff as an unburied cadaver, on top of the unkempt grave. A nest of spiders, hidden among the convolvulus, had discharged its occupants during the night to weave a blanket of silken threads across the body, guarding it against the cold as the birds had guarded the Babes in the Wood.

'Eerie it was,' said Mrs. Barnes, giving her statement down the Station, polishing up her story for the waiting press. 'Lying there white as a ghost. And smiling. I ask you. Smiling. As though she hadn't a care in the world. 'Ere, she's orlright, ain't she? Ain't gonna die?'

'Touch of hypothermia,' the Police Sergeant reassured her. 'Couple of days in the Royal Free, she'll be as right as rain.'

'What was she doing there?' asked the old lady, relief turning to bewilderment. 'In the middle of the night, in the middle of the winter?'

'Won't say' the Sergeant shrugged. 'No sign of drugs. No alcohol in the blood. It's a mystery. Grave belonged to some Victorian actress. Nobody famous.' He consulted his notebook.

'Sarah Somebody. Didn't say anything to you, I suppose, might cast some light on the proceedings?'

'Nothing as made no sense. Covered in spiders she was.' Mrs Barnes shivered at the memory. 'Thousands of the blighters running all over her. I tried to brush them off. But she didn't seem to mind one way or the other. Just sat up, with the things falling out of her hair like confetti. And what do you think she said?'

The Sergeant shook his head, waiting to be told.

'Leave 'em, she said, I'm not bothered, she said, there's worse things in this world than spiders, she said. Now what d'you suppose she could've meant by that?'

History: 'Worse Things Than Spiders', from which this anthology takes its name, was written as a two-parter for the woman's magazine Me. *They took a lot of my stuff. The then fiction editor said that when she got tired of the usual romantic fiction formula, she would say to herself—"time for another of Samantha Lee's quirky tales". When choosing material for this book I decided to "legitimise" the story, which has always been one of my favourites. But for you purists who might enquire why I should write for women's magazines in the first place, I would just say that in the early eighties, when this came out, they were paying two hundred quid for a thousand words. This means that 'Worse things' brought me in eight hundred pounds, the same amount as the advance on my first book* The Quest for the Sword of Infinity. *Sometimes, when the landlord is knocking on the door, virtue, as its own reward, simply doesn't cut it. There's also a half hour screenplay adaptation of this story up for grabs, if anybody out there is interested.*

TAKE FIVE

ZOOT SHOOK HIS head but the fuzziness remained. If it hadn't been so uncool, he might even have asked 'Where am I?' His last memory was of blowing the ultimate note in *Satin Doll*... then came the blackout.

And yet, here he was, sitting in this very plush dive (a dive wherein, he was sure, he had never before set foot) with a drink in one hand, a cheroot in the other and a tingling anticipation such as he hadn't felt since he was a kid in downtown Chicago.

'Hey man.'

Zoot looked up in surprise. A tall, dark stranger stood observing him nonchalantly. What could only have been described as a sardonic smile was plastered across his kisser.

'Hey,' said Zoot, taking the new dude in. No doubt about it, the cat was sharp... as a tack. The creases in the trousers of his pinstripe suit would have done justice to a razor and the points of his narrow lapels might easily have doubled as toothpicks. The blood-red carnation in his buttonhole was the only spot of colour in the entire tasteful collage. He was wearing a black silk shirt, a white satin tie and a dove-grey fedora. His feet were hidden by the tablecloth, but Zoot would have wagered his Sax to a penny whistle that the man was wearing spats. He was that kind of a dude.

'May I?' asked the stranger and before Zoot could say "yeah" or "neah" he had eased his elegant frame into an adjoining gilt chair. 'Drink?' he enquired politely, and Zoot said he didn't mind if he did.

The stranger pointed a perfectly manicured fingernail at Zoot's near empty glass and before his astonished eyes, the level of the corn-coloured liquid rose until it was lapping the brim.

'Now listen man...' Zoot began, but his companion casually raised a silencing hand.

'Show's about to start,' he said.

A hush fell over the crowded salon as the red velvet curtains swished back to reveal a big band dressed in scarlet and black. Pink spotlights ricocheted off their glinting instruments and threw dancing flames onto the dark orange backcloth.

Zoot's eyes began to pop as they travelled over the brass section. This surely was some line-up. In fact, the entire band consisted of the grooviest selection of heads ever collected under one roof. And yet something niggled at the back of his mind.

It wasn't until a very famous black lady singer stepped up to the microphone to enquire of the assembled throng 'Am I blue?' that the penny dropped. That particular lady singer was also very dead. As were the rest of the ensemble.

Zoot closed his eyes and abandoned himself to the sound. It was like nothing he'd ever heard before. The music lapped around his eardrums like liquid silk.

'I made it,' he whispered to himself. 'Man, I actually made it. I never had myself figured for heaven... but here I am.'

'Why don't you sit in?' suggested a smooth voice at his elbow.

Zoot shook himself out of his euphoria and found himself staring into the dark stranger's mesmeric yellow eyes.

'What me?' he gasped in awe. 'Me? Play with those cats? You gotta be joking.'

The tall dark stranger said far from it, he owned the joint and Zoot only had to say the word and he could be up there with his peers.

To Zoot's objection that he hadn't brought his Sax, he responded by producing one out of thin air. A gleaming, gold object, the like of which Zoot had never been able to afford in all his drink-sodden life. He hefted the instrument lovingly in his hands, put the reed to his mouth and blew a few practise arpeggios.

It was as though the Sax played him. Its rich, fluid tones fired Zoot's long dormant ambition and soothed any butterflies he might have felt about playing with the illustrious gathering of musicians on stage.

'Why not?' he chortled. 'What've I gotta loose?'

The trumpet player waved a welcoming had in greeting as he clambered up the rostrum steps. The band were into an up-tempo version of Zoot's all-time favourite tune—*Honeysuckle Rose*.

He joined in, playing like he'd never played before, blowing the skids from under every other Saxman there. He even took a solo, one of such brilliance that it elicited an ecstatic response from the packed audience. As one, they got to their collective feet and gave him his first ever standing ovation.

Zoot was beside himself.

The tune wound on and on, until the band had exhausted every nuance of every note, every slight and subtle variation on every theme. And then they went back and started all over again from the top.

Zoot began to flag a little. The old ticker wasn't all that it might have been. He felt that tell-tale twinge in the chest, the numbing sensation in the left arm that heralded an attack. He shuffled across to the band-leader and hissed in his ear.

'Hey man... when do we take a break?'

The trumpet player rolled his eyes in Zoot's direction. They held a hollow emptiness that made his blood run cold. For the first time since Zoot had come up onto the podium the trumpet player lowered his mouthpiece.

Blood oozed from the splits in an upper lip that was covered in half-healed sores.

'What break?' he said.

And suddenly Zoot realised that he wasn't in Heaven after all...

History: 'Take Five' took about five minutes to write, which is also how long it took for Valentine Dyall to read it on Capital Radio's Moment of Terror, *for which it was originally commissioned in 1977. The series went out at midnight and Dyall, famous for his dark brown voice and hair-raising delivery on the BBC's* Appointment with Fear, *performed it with aplomb. The station took several more of my short stories for the slot, among them 'Medium Rare' and 'Dark Reflections', both of which later appeared in print. But 'Take Five' outshone them all by a mile. Not only did it appear in Volume 8, No 15 of* Fantasy Tales *it was also snapped up by the men's magazine* Knave *and later by the women's magazine* Me—*thus covering virtually all the bases. I like to think Zoot would have been pleased.*

THE ISLAND OF THE SEALS

IT HAD BEEN an unproductive day to say the least. The constant singing of the seals out in the bay had made her strangely restless, distracting her from the task in hand. Crumpled and discarded sheets of paper overflowed the wastepaper basket. She hadn't written one cohesive paragraph since morning.

Eventually, near dusk, she gave up all pretence at concentration and crossing to the window, began to watch the sleek, grey bodies dipping and weaving far out in the still water. Like the legendary mermen of old, their tails and fins flashed in the gradually fading light. Mesmerised, she stared until the crescent moon began to rise and the vaporous tendrils of the sea-mist obscured them at their love play.

When they were completely out of sight, she turned away, carrying with her into the newly darkened room, the sound of their shrill and melancholy keening.

The night air had brought with it a sudden chill and she shivered involuntarily, pulling her shawl around her shoulders. The isolation was beginning to get her down. She craved company, missed the stimulation of human conversation. She shrugged, pulling herself back from the brink of depression and, setting the kettle to boil on the small hob, began to prepare her solitary evening meal.

Perhaps she would feel more "inspired" when she'd eaten?

She was lighting the ancient and somewhat temperamental oil-lamp when the knock sounded lightly on the door. In the silence of the Hebridean evening it had the effect of an atomic explosion and she froze in momentary shock.

At last, pulling herself together, she lifted the lamp high and moved across the small room to the half-door. A trail of grotesque, lengthening shadows draped themselves like an elaborate train of chiaroscuro folds behind her.

She undid the latch with her left hand and opened the top section of the door to waist level, swinging it in towards her and peering, as she did so, out into the garden.

Silhouetted in the picture frame shape stood a young man. The swiftly rising haa'ar, as the Islanders call the treacherous sea-fog, swirled about his head like a horse's breath on a frosty day. Behind him the shingle path leading down to the beach, lay shrouded in secrecy.

She judged him to be about twenty five years old, tall and tanned, with thick brown hair, sleek and shining as though damp from the sea. His eyes were brown too, fringed with long, dark lashes. But his most striking feature was the ears. Small for a man, they lay, curled like fine pink shells, flat to his head.

He spoke, greeting her in the lilting tones of the Gaelic, with a voice that was at once soft and hypnotic. He wished her health and many blessings. He said he had seen her standing by the window and had been reminded of how long it had been since he had heard a human voice. And she, remembering that the custom of the Islands demanded hospitality be offered to anyone, friend or stranger, whom chance might bring to the door, bade him enter and sit awhile.

She gave him milk and oatcakes with honey and they talked long into the night. He knew much of the folklore of the outer isles, stories she had never heard before. The curious, soporific quality of his voice as he recounted to her magical tales of death and enchantment, lulled her into a semi-coma of content.

Sitting opposite to him in the flickering firelight seemed the most natural thing in the world, as though all her life she had been expecting his arrival, as though for the first time in her small, drab existence, she had discovered something worthwhile.

He reached forward to touch her hand and to her surprise she did not draw it away, but curled her fingers around his and put her other hand up to stroke the thick dark hair and fondle the strange small ears.

He looked at her, long and deep, his eyes as dark as rock-pools in the bay. She felt the blood rush to her face and her limbs took on a strange lightness as she read in his gaze the promise of an end and a beginning. She stood up, stumbling in her agitation and he placed his hand on her arm to steady her. His grip sent a surge of feeling through her body, which left her incapable of resistance as he led her quietly through the open door into the tiny bedroom.

Next morning, when she woke to the sound of the soft, insistent chanting of the seals among the rocks, he had gone. Only the mark of his head on the pillow remained to assure her that he had been there at all.

She waited for evening in a fine fury of apprehension, wishing the warm spring day away. Unable to concentrate on her writing, she paced the room, hugging herself, as the memories of the night flooded back in waves of emotion that made her head whirl.

By the time the sun had set, what remained of her pride was in shreds and when at last his light tap echoed on the half-door, she flung herself at him, crying in relief.

And it was as though he'd never gone, for he stilled her fears with his kisses, holding her in the circle of his arms until she fell asleep against his strong dark body.

So it continued all through the late spring and early summer, her love deepening and growing, while in the background the ever -present seal colony thrived like grain in the ripening sun.

In the beginning she questioned him about his daily absences but he merely smiled and changed the subject, so that eventually she began to accept his reticence as a fact of their life together and ceased her enquiries.

Every morning he had disappeared as usual and her days were her own. She had given up all pretence of writing now. Her sense of unreality in the daylight hours increased as the months went by. Her love had become an obsession and she lived only for the nights, existed in a sort of waking dream while she awaited the return of her solitary, secret lover and their dark hours together.

To pass the time between sunrise and sunset she would take long walks on the beach where the seal community had their home. She watched the small, furry pups growing under their mother's constant care, the great bulls fighting to retain their territory, the young males trying out their growing strength in mock battles.

She felt an affinity with the seals that she had never had with her own kind. She had always been an outsider, a loner, considered slightly odd because she had no interest in the grasping opportunism that had taken over humanity. It was one of the reasons she had begun to write. It gave her an excuse, a reason to enjoy her solitude unharrassed by the thoughtless, wounding, insinuating gossip that had hounded her childhood and teens.

Now, on the island, she had found the perfect balance. By day the seals gave her companionship without intrusion and by night she loved and was loved unconditionally in return. True, she wasn't doing any work. But there would be plenty of time for that afterwards. And she didn't want to think of afterwards yet. Even though she knew in her heart of hearts that somewhere, sometime, the magical summer had to end.

It was the first week in September that the boat arrived, a powerful boat carrying four powerful men. She watched them from the window as they landed and made camp among the rocks, covering the virgin shingle with a disorderly pile of accoutrements: tarpaulins and lengths of rope, a battered kettle, a primus stove.

They brewed some tea and sat in a circle drinking it and laughing together. Their harsh, mainland accents mingled with the intoxicating scent of newly blooming gorse, to drift through her open window.

The tallest of the men stood up and bent over the fire to refill his cup. As he straightened, the sun glinted briefly on the knife in his belt, and behind her curtain she felt her skin turn cold with the realisation of why they had come.

It was time for the "culling".

Somewhere, far away in so-called civilisation, the "authorities" had decided that the number of seals must be kept strictly in check. Because of the fishing. Faceless men, who had never even seen the colony, had condemned half of it to death. And the four "conservationists" before her would have paid well for the privilege of butchering hundreds of helpless, trusting animals. For seal-skins brought a small fortune on the black market and the licence to cull would be priced accordingly, everybody turning a blind eye.

The four men finished their tea, throwing the dregs onto the sun-bleached stones and stacking the enamel cups in an untidy heap by the primus stove, for future reference.

Then they wiped their hands, rolled up their sleeves and systematically began the slaughter.

In the grip of a horrible fascination, she watched as they skinned the half grown pups and young males. They worked methodically, their long handled clubs rising and falling rhythmically, careful only to strike the skull so that the pelt should not be damaged. Some they killed outright: the lucky ones. Some they skinned while they were only half dead or stunned.

For two hours she gazed ashen-faced, unable to tear her eyes away from the carnage, feeling sick to her stomach. And all the time the pile of bloody skins mounted.

At last the "head man" raised an arm, elbow deep in gore, to call a halt.

As though nothing had happened, the evening sunlight continued to illuminate a beach littered with blood and viscera, like the aftermath of a great battle.

In the shadow of a large outcropping of rock a seal mother leant whimpering over what was left of her offspring. Nudging it gently with her flippers she tried to push the pathetic scrap of exposed muscle and sinew towards the safety of the sea.

The cullers rinsed their carmine stained hands and began to prepare an evening meal. They ate ravenously, totally oblivious to the devastation all around them.

She turned from the window and lay down on the bed, her body weak with anguish and disgust. From outside she could hear the plaintive bleating of the seals, punctuated by the coarse laughter of the men. And she wept with shame for humanity. For its needless cruelty and senseless greed. Wept until she had no more tears. Turning her face to the wall.

Gradually the sky darkened and the autumn evening closed around her. Exhausted by her distress, her eyelids began to droop over eyes ravaged by the afternoon's atrocities and she drifted thankfully into oblivion.

She woke to total darkness. Total darkness and a deafening silence. A pang of terror gripped her, followed by an overpowering sense of foreboding. For she was alone. Tonight, when she needed his strength as never before, he hadn't come.

Feeling her way haltingly in the darkness, she crossed to the window. The crescent moon hung, a slice of melon under frosted glass, almost obscured by the sea-mist.

It was a night like that first night had been. The only difference was that now and then the warning light of the alien boat winked on and off, a scarlet pinprick amongst the filigree of fog.

A primitive urge, stronger than she could contain, compelled her towards the beach. Lifting her shawl from where she had flung it earlier, she threw it round her thin shoulders and stumbled out into the mist.

The haa'ar came and went in dense clumps as she picked her way down the shingle to the shore. She trudged on blindly, completely losing all sense of direction, tripping on rocks, slipping on seaweed, only saved from occasionally walking into the sea by the cyclopean winking of the seal-culler's light.

And with each step the feeling became stronger. Terror and grief intermingled, guiding her towards some nameless destination in the fog-wrapped shroud of the night.

The compulsion had been leading her on in this aimless fashion for almost an hour and she was chilled to the bone when a huge rock loomed out of the mist in front of her. And there, in the lee of its overhang, she finally found him. His naked shoulder, as she bent to touch him, felt cold and oddly sticky. Nauseated by the sensation, she drew back her hand. It was covered in blood. She leant forward to observe him more closely.

The back of his head had been battered to a pulp.

Controlling her mounting revulsion with great effort, she knelt down and turned him over on his back. The sudden shock of what

28

she saw made her clamp her blood-soaked hand over her mouth in an attempt to still the hysterical screams bubbling up in her throat, threatening to engulf what was left of her sanity.

There wasn't an inch of skin left on him. Skin or hair. He'd been completely scalped and his beautiful ears had been severed from his head. His dark eyes that had looked on her with such tenderness were covered in a white film of death and stared up at her like those of a cod on a fishmongers slab.

The first wave of horror was superseded by an unimaginable wave of grief. So deep and intense was her agony that she felt she was being physically torn in two.

Gathering the flayed corpse to her chest, she began to keen, a high, continuous crooning moan. And as her wailing mounted in pitch, she started to rock, backwards and forwards, like a mother trying to soothe a fractious child to sleep. The tempo of her rocking increased and her tone took on a higher, whining quality as she pressed her face to what was left of his, heedless of the blood which stained her clothing and coagulated in her wild hair.

And as she wailed, she began to hear, like an echo swirling through the mists over the still waters of the bay, soft voices raised to join in her lament. Comforting voices, whispering to her of the cool, green depths of the bottomless channel where the seals forever glide among the swaying seaweed forests. Voices beckoning her to where the dark, limpet-encrusted rock caverns know no sound but the singing of the seal-maiden to her sleek, grey love. Calling her away from a world grown too terrible to bear. Calling her home.

She raised her head and ceased to rock, sniffing the salt air like a dog that has scented its prey. Then her tortured eyes cleared and she smiled.

'Wait for me,' she called.

And bending tenderly to kiss the broken skull for the last time, she gently eased the tattered remains of her lost love onto the shingle.

As she stood unsteadily on her feet, the red light from the boat winked on, glistening her bloodstained mouth momentarily in the dark. Absentmindedly, she pushed the dishevelled hair away from her face and, clutching the shawl to her thin body, she walked slowly and deliberately into the black, mist-enshrouded waters.

Notice in the *Edinburgh Examiner*

November 25th 1988

The inquest was held today on the death of Miss Moira Spencer, whose body was found last September, washed up on the beach of Seal Island, the wildlife sanctuary in the Outer Hebrides.

Miss Spencer, who was sixty-one years old and a spinster had taken a cottage for the summer on the otherwise uninhabited island, to complete the writing of her fantasy novel, "The Seal People". The book was to be based on the old legends incorporating the belief held by many Hebrideans, that the seals are an enchanted race possessing the power to assume human form during the hours of darkness.

Miss Spencer's body, which was discovered by a group of "cullers" working in the area, was thought to have been in the water for several days.

She is survived by an elderly aunt.

Coroner's Verdict: Death by misadventure.

History: This story was written during my Celtic Twilight period when I was living in the north of Scotland and fascinated by all things fey. Standing stones on uninhabited islands that turned into dancing maidens at full moon; demon lovers who spirited their way into virgin bedrooms at midnight; fairy forts a-bustle with the little people; water horses (think Loch Ness); changelings; Finn folk and druidic sacrifice—a veritable cornucopia of inspirational material. About the same time I wrote 'The Selkie's Cap' for Fantasy Stories, *edited by Mike Ashley. 'The Lilac Tree', published in 'Me' covered the Demon Lover angle and an evil spirit allegedly lurking at crossroads at 'dark o' the moon' led to my Scholastic Point Horror novel* The Bogle. *The late Herbert Van Thal, bless his cotton socks, used 'The Island of the Seals' in* The 18th Pan Book of Horror Stories. *It was then chosen by Charlie Grant for his* Final Shadows *and has since been translated into German as 'Die Robbinsel' and into Spanish for inclusion in* Horropatia *published by the Barcelona editorial 'Tyrannosaurus'. In hindsight I have a sneaking suspicion that some of these folktales may have been fuelled by a surfeit of lampreys washed down with copious drams of the Glenfiddich. But what the hell, whatever gets you through the (long northern winter) night, right?*

JELLY ROLL BLUES

THE BARMAID, A pulchritudinous piece in her late twenties, polishing glasses with all the application of the terminally bored, looked up in surprise as Pete came in shaking the snow off his trench-coat.

'What a night,' he said, ankling through the deep pile carpet to perch on a stool at the bar. 'Give us a double brandy, love, and have one for yourself, will you?'

The barmaid, who gloried in the name of Raquel, favoured Pete with a toothsome smile.

'Don't mind if I do, handsome,' she said. 'I'll have a G and T if it's all the same to you?'

'Make it a large one,' said Pete, all generosity. 'After all, it IS Christmas Eve.'

Raquel turned her attention to the relevant optics and Pete noted with appreciation, the pleasing spectacle of the barmaid's voluptuous bottom struggling to escape from its skin-tight satin sheath.

'Quiet tonight,' he observed, swivelling in his seat to get a better view of the premises.

Understatement of the year. Pete was the only person in the place. And he was damned if he could figure out why? Because the Holly Bush, on a drinking man's pub scale of one to ten, undoubtedly rated a good nine and three quarters.

The lighting was muted, the music mellow, the atmosphere warm and welcoming. The plush chairs were well padded (like Raquel) and astrew with plump cushions that almost begged to be relaxed in. The panelled walls, hung with horse-brasses and hunting prints, smelled faintly of polish, as did the dark oak tables, each complete with a gleaming ashtray and to hell with political correctness. In one corner, an enormous log fire crackled cheerily, the light from its flames reflecting, like coloured fireflies, in the baubles on the adjacent Christmas tree. In short, the Holly Bush was what every tavern should be, but frequently was not. A veritable home from home. A place where a man could chill out at the end of a long, hard day. The total antithesis in fact, of those juke-boxed, neon-lit, pin-ball machine polluted theme dumps, awash with Mexican beer and unpleasant company, which so often posed as public houses in these so-called enlightened times.

'Always quiet,' Raquel confided, morosely.

She plonked the serving of dark gold Courvoisier in front of her solitary customer and leant her elbows on the counter, affording Pete a grandstand view of her ample breasts. Firelight flickered in the pupils of her whiskey coloured eyes and Pete reflected that, as the Holly Bush was to pubs, so Raquel was to barmaids—well-nigh perfect.

'Can't understand it,' he said, lifting his glass to salute her before allowing the smooth spirit to slick down his throat. 'Nice pub. Nice company.' He winked and Raquel had the good grace to blush, taking a hasty sip of gin and tonic to cover her confusion. 'Nice brandy.' Pete had another swallow to prove his point. 'What's the problem? Place ought to be bursting at the seams.'

'Don't I know it,' pouted Raquel. 'Used to be too. Then the Rose and Garter down the road pinched our piano player. Offered him more money if you please and he just upped and left, taking all the customers with him.'

She tossed her raven locks in scorn at such disloyalty and Pete tut-tutted his disapproval, remembering the saloon he had passed at the far end of the street. It had, indeed, been bulging with seasonal revellers and a maudlin voice, crucifying "My Way", had filtered out through the dirty windows to the accompaniment of a tinny piano.

'Now I won't get my Christmas bonus,' said Raquel, plaintively, and a tear welled in her big brown eyes and fell with a plop onto her cleavage.

Pete wiped it away with his handkerchief, lingering slightly longer than was absolutely necessary under the circumstances.

Raquel's breath, warm and sweetened with the scent of juniper berries, fanned his cheek with the promise of infinite possibilities.

'We'd better do something about that,' announced Pete.

So saying, he groped in the cavernous pocket of his trench-coat and produced, rather as a magician might spirit a rabbit from a hat, a tiny little mannequin.

Raquel's luscious mouth dropped open and her wide eyes stretched even wider. As a barmaid of some experience, she'd seen many a strange sight in her day, but never anything to compare with this small but perfectly formed homunculus, immaculately clad in white tie and tails and smoking a strong cheroot. He stood just slightly over a foot tall.

'Hi gorgeous,' said the apparition. 'You got a piano in this joint?'

'In the corner,' croaked Raquel and proceeded to award herself another double gin, double quick.

Pete meanwhile, delighted at the effect he was having, crossed to the baby grand, raised the lid, and deposited his miniscule companion on the keys.

As soon as his toes touched middle C the little chap began to play, tripping the light fantastic in a manner not unreminiscent of a miniature Fred Astaire. He twirled and pranced, sashayed and do-se-doed, bucking and winging up and down the instrument like a tiny, tapping, terpsichorean tornado.

And the sound he produced was sheer magic.

The mellifluous mood-music circled the salon, caressing the ear like liquid silk. Then it meandered out into the snow-clad street, a siren call beckoning the unwary traveller from the straight and narrow.

Before he had finished the second chorus of "Putting on the Ritz", the first customers had begun to trickle in.

An hour later, the place was jammed.

By the end of the evening Raquel had had to S.O.S. several times for extra bar staff and more beer and her Christmas bonus was assured—in triplicate.

Later... much later... having disposed of the more immediate urgencies, Raquel turned over on her side and posed Pete the question she'd been dying to ask all evening.

'Where on earth did you find him?'

Pete glanced contentedly towards the dressing-table drawer, where the little piano man snored soundly amongst Raquel's unmentionables.

'Funny story that,' he said. 'Happened on Christmas Eve, strangely enough. Couple of years ago now. Centre of Oxford Street. Usual crush of last minute shoppers. Bedlam to tell the truth. Traffic was murder. Anyway, there was me, just about to cross the road, when I spot this old bloke, falling apart at the seams he was, dithering about on the kerb, scared to go over. So I gave him a hand, didn't I?

'And guess what? When we got to the other side he looked at me—sly like—and he says...

'"Young man, that's the first act of human kindness that's been shown me in many a long year. I'm not really an old tramp," he says, "as you might have supposed from my appearance. Actually," he says, "I'm Father Christmas and, as a reward, you can have one wish. Name it. Anything your heart desires..."

'And maybe it was because the traffic was so loud... or perhaps the old codger was a bit hard of hearing... whatever... I ended up with a thirteen inch pianist!'

History: Someone, I can't remember who, told me this joke at a British Fantasy Society open night (or, if you prefer, booze-up) so it seems apposite that it was included in Fantasy Tales 2, *the second volume after the publication moved from small press into the more expanded version put out by Robinson.*

SILENT SCREAM

THE RATS ERUPTED from the wainscotting, big, fat hairy things with tails pink as unlinked sausages. They skittered across the floor in a tidal surge, feral eyes shiny as skinned grapes in the light-bulb's naked glare.

She wriggled in the restraining jacket, trying to press back into the wall, tearing feverishly at the inside of the sleeves with quick-bitten fingernails. Her feet made little kicking patterns, crumpling the hospital smooth bedlinen, ripping it out of its carefully folded corners.

When the whiskers appeared, light as thistledown, over the edge of the cot, she began to whimper, veins cording her neck, legs suddenly damp with the spurt of unretainable urine. The warm, salt smell, more aromatic than blood, reached the nose of the pack leader. He halted a hand-span from her naked ankle and sat up, sniffing the air.

Behind him, his minions clambered over the counterpane in a sea of ululating flesh, the souls of other, earlier victims staring out of the bright eyes as if to say... 'Your turn, your turn.'

'Go away, go away,' she shrieked in her fiercest, loudest voice.

But the chief rat only smiled, curling pink lips back over pinker gums, dropping on all fours and ducking under the ward-issue gown, to run up her leg and sink sharp white fangs into the soft, exposed flesh of her inside thigh.

Blood spurted, pumping from the vein in her groin.

No pain. Not yet. Just disbelief—and the sound of her voice screaming as the rest of the monsters swarmed up to cover her in a blanket of squirming bodies.

'Jesus H Christ... what's going on?'

The cell door opening, two men in white coats rushing in. Salvation. She wept with relief as none too gently, one held her down while the other administered the injection.

The rats scattered at the men's approach, disappearing into the white walls, melting back through the floor while the hole through which they had so mysteriously emerged closed over. The Red Sea engulfing the cream of Rameses' Charioteers.

She lay back, body soaked in sweat and piss, sinking down into the blessed blackness of the drug, the coarse faces of her deliverers swimming out of vision, voices grumbling about the mess that would have to be cleared up yet again.

CASTELLI. Worst case of DT's I ever seen. Look at the way she's squirming around in there. You'd think something was eatin' her alive.

PETROWSKI. The demon drink, Charlie, the demon drink. She's been tippling for years. Be sure you're sins will find you out. You ought to know that, Charlie, you being good catholic and all.

CASTELLI. How come a nice old lady like that gets to drinking in the first place? Nice home, nice family, nice life. I don't geddit.

PETROWSKI. Maybe it ain't always been so nice. Old man Glassier says she was in one of them camps during the war. Maybe she drinks to forget?

CASTELLI. Lotta crap talked about them camps y'ask me. Could'na been as bad as they said. Old lady like that, peeing her pants. It ain't seemly.

PETROWSKI. She ain't so old. In her sixties. Says so in her notes.

CASTELLI. Jesus, she looks eighty if she looks a day.

PETROWSKI. Yeah, well, the booze ain't too good for the complexion, Charlie boy.

CASTELLI. Ain't too good for the sheets neither. Nice old lady like that. You think she'd be ashamed.

For a moment she was at peace.

Then the dreams started. Dreams worse than the hallucinations. Closer to reality. Harder to bear.

It was the winter of '42. She was sixteen and back at the camp.

The rats were there too. They had eaten the foot off a three day old baby before the mother, a girl not much older than herself, had woken from the sleep of starvation and beaten them off in a frenzy of hate and fear.

The child had died soon after, from shock and loss of blood. And the mother, a stick figure with huge shadowed eyes, ugly in her grief, had gone insane, clutching the wizened scrap to her milkless breasts until the flesh turned putrid and began to dribble down the front of her prison issue tunic.

All this had taken time. But in the dream it happened instanta-neously, the baby's body melting into green slime punctuated by pockets of putridness which exploded into small ulcerated craters and from which inch long worms, wriggled their way onto the mother's emaciated chest.

One morning the woman too had been dead, the child still clutched to her bosom. They had buried them later that afternoon—if you could call it burial—thrown into a common pit, covered in quick lime to keep the plague away.

It had been a beautiful morning in early May. They say there are no birds at Auschwitz. But birds had been singing that day as they'd tipped mother and child into the trench.

Mozart had fared no better.

But at least he hadn't had to put up with the rats.

Rats everywhere, thriving on dead flesh, sharpening their teeth on human bones, turning on each other when the corpses got too skinny, cycling and re-cycling themselves in an obscene orgy of cannibalistic gluttony.

It was her horror of the rats, her fear of what they might do to her after she was dead that made her decide to live at all costs.

TRANSCRIPT OF INTERVIEW BETWEEN MRS. IRMA LONGFORD AND JOHN PAUL GLASSIER, RESIDENT PSYCHIATRIST, MOUNTVILLE STATE PSYCHIATRIC UNIT, NEW STANTON USA.

<u>DR G</u>. You understand, don't you Mrs. Longford, that your drinking is only symptomatic of some other, deeper problem?

(SILENCE)

<u>DR G</u>. (ctd) Mrs. Longford. We can't help you unless you help yourself. We know you've been through a bad time. But it's over now. It's been over for fifty years. Maybe if you talked about it you could, you know, lay the ghost?

(SILENCE)

<u>DR G</u>. (ctd) Mrs. Longford. I know this is hard for you. Often, when things happen... like happened to you... deprivation... a feeling of life being out of control, it leaves us scarred, ashamed even, because we didn't behave...perhaps... as well as we ought. There can even be guilt about being alive when others died. It's a common trauma. We often see it in the wake of a natural disaster. An earthquake for instance or a tsunami. After the relief wears off people are often left with a hollow feeling. 'Why me?' they say. 'Why did SHE die while I'm still here?' Some individuals go mad under the strain, get strange notions, in extreme cases persuade themselves that they've somehow been the cause of the disaster, that it's their fault so many others died. I had one man in here, after an airline crash, who was convinced that he'd somehow made a pact with the Devil, that he'd sold his soul, that THAT was the only reason he was still alive. Guilt is understandable. It's a post-traumatic symptom. But therapy can help Mrs. Longford. If you'd only just co-operate, talk about it. This is not the dark ages. We can help you. But we need you to meet us half way.

(SILENCE

<u>DR G</u>. (sighing) Very well, Mrs. Longford. If you won't co-operate, I can't make you, though I can't understand why you won't try. If you won't think about yourself, think about your children... your grandchildren. Think how hard it is for them to watch you go through this. Their sympathy could go a long way to helping you to a permanent cure. They love you Mrs. Longford. Wouldn't it be better all round if they knew the truth?

(MUFFLED LAUGHTER, CHILLING IN ITS LACK OF HUMOUR)

<u>DR G</u>. (stiffly) Right Mrs. Longford. It seems there's no more to be said. Your son will be here in a few minutes to sign the release

form. (Sound of papers being shuffled) And remember Mrs. Longford, you're a hopeless alcoholic. If you ever drink again, you'll die, do you understand?

She sat by the window, smocking a dress for Marsha's youngest. The needle flew, in and out, in and out, piercing the flesh-coloured silk into a series of knots and ridges The puckered pattern brought to mind the scars of those inmates who'd undergone the human vivisection (No anaesthetic naturally, Jews weren't human, after all, and one needed the chloroform and drugs for our brave soldiers on the front). She shook the thought away concentrating instead on her hands. Wrinkled as they were and marked with blotches brought on by too many winters spent in Miami while Jack was still alive, they were as nimble as they had been when she was sixteen years old. She had been sewing the night the soldiers had come and dragged them from the house. Loud voices and louder boots clamping on the cobbles in the lamplight. And the neighbours, peering through the windows, glad it wasn't them. 'Never did like those Varmann's anyway. Too uppity.' Sewing linen for her bottom drawer in anticipation of a normal sixteen year olds future. Marriage and children. Happy ever after.

She looked again at the silk, mind hooking onto items sewn long ago, in afternoons while Blucher snored and she, plagued with nightmares even then, would leave her lover asleep to search the bodies of the dead for anything the guards might have missed. A button perhaps or a piece of string. That body, stumbled over, still clinging to life. The eyes, staring from the half-eaten face (the rats again) begging for release. A sudden moment of forgotten tenderness and the hiss of the life-force escaping the punctured lung as she drove the sewing scissors home. The gratitude in the eyes as the light died. So unlike those other eyes, the rats eyes of her dreams, reflecting the thousand upon thousands of souls, driven to the long barrows, expecting the kiss of hot showers, blessed relief from the vermin that had flourished in the cattle-wagons, receiving instead the acrid embrace of gas filling the chambers.

'I am become death', she thought, fingers flying, wondering why she hadn't used the scissors to kill herself.

Those who HAD died, climbing over the bodies of their own children to claw at the doors, were the lucky ones.

For the rest, the slow torture of starvation, slave labour, or worse... collusion, enjoyment even... absolute power corrupts... What became of the human soul under such conditions? She looked out at her grandchildren, playing on the lawn, their bright laughter hanging like angel choirs on the clear autumn air.

There were some who believed that the soul grew stronger under duress, that the greatest feats of heroism took place in the dirt and deprivation of the worlds torture cells.

She knew better. In the stink of the camps humanity sank to rat-level, inmates willing to betray any confidence, invent any blasphemy, commit any act in order to survive another day.

Some had even been known to sell a virgin daughter to a camp guard for a lump of sour bread.

Out of the corner of her eye she saw the head appear round the leg of the sofa. She hadn't had a drink in days, but there was another one under the table, and a third, slithering out from behind the curtain, flat as a blintz, inflating itself balloon-like before scuttling in a sideways jig towards her.

She jumped up, flinging the sewing from her, clambering unsteadily onto the rocking chair, beating at the air with clawed hands as the rodents scurried up her nylons, tiny paws puncturing fabric and flesh, seeking purchase in their inexorable climb towards her throat.

'Hello. George. Is that you? Can you come home, dear? I'm afraid it's your mother. She's had another one of her turns. Yes. I KNOW you're in the middle of a meeting...but it's more serious this time... No. No, I'm quite sure. There isn't a drop in the house... She's in bed now. She's paralyzed down one side and she can't speak. The Doctor says she's had a stroke and she may have another...You'd better come home, George (crying)... I've had to send for Father Flynn.'

Bless me, Father for I have sinned. It's been forty years since my last confession.

When I took the faith, Jack said it didn't matter what I'd done. I could confess and it'd be all right. I never did, of course. Saved it up for the end. And now I can't talk. Whoever said life was fair? I've paid my dues. I've been a good mother, a good wife. We're different people when were young. We can change. I've done my bit. And I've been punished. Every day waiting for the knock on the door. The dreams. The rats.

The ones who died deserved to, weak, gutless, pathetic. Begging to be tortured, longing for it. Victor and victim, master and slave, the good and the evil, opposite ends of the spectrum. You with your beads and your mumbo jumbo. Isn't it bad to be so weak, so stupid, placing your fate in the hands of others, begging for death, hungering for pain? And isn't there something fine... Holy almost, about inflicting it?

Torture is the oldest art. The most basic to our nature. Orchestrating the note of the scream, thin and high for exquisite pain, deep and vomit-gurgling for agony.

And the power... holding them there... like God, between life and death, allowing them to die... eventually, because by then they want to, because life is too hideous to contemplate without eyes or breasts or genitalia.

Bless me, Father for I have sinned.

I have my mother to thank I suppose? - weak, silly woman. I might never have realized my penchant for pain if she hadn't sold me to that pig, Blucher. He took me to the cells to frighten me, to show me what would happen if I didn't perform. But I wasn't frightened, just curious, and aroused, I suppose. He got more than his bread's-worth later on.

Afterwards he took me because it pleased me, excited us both. And because I came up with such good suggestions. Kindred spirits. But he was a pig all the same. Ham-fisted. No finesse. And he died like a pig too, torn limb from limb when the war was over and the allies were at the gates.

Those allied soldiers. So naive. Jack even crying for what I'd suffered at Blucher's hand. And all those who knew the truth too dead to tell.

Mrs. Longford, respectable war-bride. Pillar of the community. Living example of the finer family values. Such a NICE old lady.

The damn rats have been the only fly in the ointment. And now there's something even worse. Lately I've started to decipher a sort of twittering among their squeaks, like a Radio turned down low. Voices without words, just below the level of comprehension. As though any minute now they're going to start to talk. To cry out. To accuse.

Amazing how humanity clings to life. Why? When what follows can be no worse than what they leave behind. I've seen life held in limbo inside a lump of flesh until it was no more than that, a flayed, disfigured mound of guts and sinew with no throat left to voice its silent screams, no tongue left to thank me when I persuaded my lover to let it die.

In those days death was the most natural thing in the world. Living was hard. Still is. Death is my salvation. Away from the rats of cannibal conscience.

Absolve me Father, you in your black shroud...absolve me, now and at the hour... Give me peace.

Oh Holy Mother of God what IS this? The black cassock sprouting hair, whiskers slithering out of the pores, nose lengthening, twitching, sniffing, thirsty for blood. Keep your claws off me. Don't touch me. Stay away. Stay away...

Poor tortured woman, thought Father Flynn, what had she gone through, what memories would she carry with her to the grave? He leant forward and placed his hands on the narrow shoulders, pressing the frail old bones back into the crisp linen pillowcase.

Her eyes looked out at him in abject terror, toothless mouth gaping, spittle drooling. A wicked looking old face, he thought, immediately ashamed that such a thing should have sprung to mind, so unlike that of the innocent eighteen year old who's portrait smiled from the mantelpiece, safe at last on the arm of the man who had found her in the filth of the concentration camp and brought her to America to be his wife.

Irma Longford screamed once and fell back, and Father Flynn, feeling his own weight of years heavy on him, allowed his head to sink on his chest and wondered about the meaning of if all.

Later at the graveside, he would speak of her many qualities, of the good she had done during her time on earth, of her humanity, her loving family who would miss her and the fact that, without her, the world would be an emptier place.

'She is at peace now', he would say, piously. 'Gone to her just reward.'

She woke in total darkness, the air damp and warm, tinged with a smell not unlike the foul fumes that had belched from the smoke-stacks daily above the gas-chambers.

Under her back she could feel the earth shuddering as though somewhere, beneath her day-old corpse a dormant volcano was preparing to erupt into life.

She had won. The struggle was over. The rats had gone. They couldn't touch her now. She felt as though a huge weight had been lifted from her soul.

So this was Heaven. Back to the womb. Nothingness. Emptiness. Peace.

In the darkness, a face swam before her. Mother's face, the eyes dark and beautiful, her throaty voice lulling the six year old Irma to sleep with a song in Yiddish.

The ground ceased its shuddering and began to heave. It bucked like a bronco in the darkness, tossing her from side to side, bouncing her off the satin shell of the casket as she'd once flung herself from wall to wall in the padded cell.

A sharp protrusion dug into her back. A jagged splinter of wood. An earthquake? Something was trying to get in, burrowing up through the bottom of the coffin.

Before she heard the scrabbling of the soft furry paws or heard the murmur of the far-away voices, she knew what it was and she screeched like a banshee, trying to sit up, banging her head, falling back again half-stunned. Desperately she rolled over onto her stomach and heaved, pushing at the unyielding wood with her narrow shoulders, trying to angle her way out through the lid and hold the floor together at the same time. Anything to stop them getting in, getting at her.

A hole opened beneath her. An abyss. She couldn't see it but she could feel the soft, wet nose, the tickle of whiskers under her palm. And the voices louder now calling up dark memories in the dark. Her mother, apologizing, begging for mercy, the twins, deliberately infected with rabies, screaming obscenities as they tore each other's faces off, her best friend's shriek as the aborted foetus slithered from her butchered body, Blucher calling her name, turning accusing eyes on her as she joined his murderers helping to rip his body to shreds.

The rats burst through the coffin, bringing with them the red glow of Hell's cauldron. And in that glow she saw that they were no ordinary rats. Instead of animal heads, they had human faces, human voices, a human desire for revenge.

She had one brief glimpse of her mother the last time she'd seen her, face half eaten before she'd plunged the scissors in. And then the surge of furry bodies swarmed over her, burrowing into her armpits, her groin, her mouth, silencing forever the scream that she knew would flow from her torn throat for all eternity.

History: So how far would you go to survive? And once you got there, would you allow yourself to get away with it? In other words, what are consciences for? And is there really such a thing as cosmic justice? These were the thoughts that prompted me to write 'Silent Scream'. I still don't know. It was commissioned for The Anthology of Fantasy and the Supernatural *and later included in the* Giant Book *of same. To tell you the truth, I was glad to be shot of it. But I recently saw a French movie called* Sophie's Eyes, *starring Kirsten Scott Thomas, which covered similar ground. If you feel like having your withers wrung, I recommend it. To me horror is not about monsters and mad axemen. It's about finding out that the nice bloke you've been living with for twenty years is really a serial killer. Or that your granny is something even worse.*

SCOOP

THE HEAT WAS intolerable, as it was every day. The slime that passed for water round the dilapidated landing stage crawled and hummed with a mass of insect and reptilian life, each preying one upon the other.

The fat man emptied his slop bucket into the oozing sludge and shambled the few yards along the rickety jetty to the decaying building at the river's edge, on whose rotting sign the legend "Casa Pepita" was etched in sunfaded script.

'Eh, Gordo, get a move on. You taking a siesta or what? Time you swept out the bar. We gotta make the place nice for the customers.'

The greasy, half-caste woman on the porch scratched her damp armpit reflectively. She looked at the man under heavy eyelids. He was a puzzle, that one. He had been with her for nearly twenty year and still she knew nothing about him. He had just appeared out of the jungle one day and asked, in bad Spanish, if he could stay and work for his keep. Her man was newly buried and the fat one, for he had been fat even then, though nothing like as fat as he was now, had seemed harmless enough. And it was always some protection to have a man around the place. Even a figure of fun such as this one.

She had been glad of him when the baby came. Without him she would have died too. He had even cried over the pathetic bundle with the head too big for its body. Cried. Like a woman. Strange.

Stranger still, after all this time, he remained curiously out of place. He never mixed with the men who came to the bar, put up with their insults, drank much but talked little. His Spanish, such as it was, carried the unmistakable twang of the "gringo".

And yet from his looks, he could have passed for a local. Darkly tanned by the South American sun, he had the full lips and slightly flattened nose of a native. His puffy skin, underlaid with the jaundiced tinge of alcohol abuse, was touched here and there with the scabs of old sores. His mouth hung slack under the Zapata moustache and his greasy hair, which he wore long at the sides and neck, had thinned over the crown. Sunken eyes, dark raisins in a pudding face, held the vacant expression of one who has seen too much and lived too long. He sweated in the heat like a pig.

Pepita had seen that bloated body wracked with tortuous dreams and then he would wake suddenly, eyes bulging, forehead slicked with the sweat of terror, screaming for the world to 'let him alone'.

The man limped wordlessly past, turning sideways to avoid brushing against her. Then, taking an almost hairless broom from behind the door, he began to scrape the huge black beetles from one end of the fly-blown Cantina to the other.

A few miles away, deep in the jungle, Jack Mack had struck trouble again.

He was an easy-going man, Heaven knew. All he wanted was a quiet life, a permanent seat in "El Vino's" and a nice amenable little secretary in a mini skirt. He couldn't understand what he was doing in this Godforsaken sinkhole, up to his gaiters in mud and mosquitoes. Yes he could too. It was all his new Editor's fault. Anthony Drummond. The scourge of Fleet Street. He of the acid tongue and the circulation obsession.

'Face it, Jack', he had said, during that fateful interview. 'You're not exactly our ace reporter any more. Unless you can come up with a scoop of some sort, we won't be able to carry your stuff after Christmas. It's stale, Jack, dull, no spark. But just to show you I'm a fair and reasonable man, I'm going to give you one last chance. I'm sending you to South America to do an in-depth bit on the rain-forests. I'll show those bastards that say we're a glorified scandal sheet, that the *Sporting Sunday* has the best interests of the great British public at heart.

'And while you're over there,' he went on, 'all expenses paid, see if you can come up with something saleable for Christ's sake.

Something that'll put the *Sporting Sunday* in the editorial front-line.'

'Like what?' Jack had mumbled.

'Like a Presidential assassination. Or an Inca lost city. Use your imagination man, you're a newspaperman aren't you?'

Jack squashed a mosquito between forefinger and thumb and bridled at the memory.

Supercilious bastard. What did he know about newspapermen? A bloody yuppie. A man who spent his lunchtime in the gym, for Christ's sake. A man who drank Perrier water.

'Maybe I could find fuckin' Hitler', Jack said, taking a swig from his hip flask and toying with the idea of sending Drummond a poisonous snake through the post.

'Come on Paco,' he bawled, as his local guide struggled to lever the hired car out of the mirey track where it had become inextricably imbedded for the fourth time since what had laughingly passed for breakfast in this hell-hole. 'We ain't got all day, you know?'

As far as Jack Mack was concerned the quicker they destroyed the blasted rain-forests the better. If he wanted bleeding foliage he could get it in Highgate Cemetery. It would be opening time in The Spaniards, he reflected, morosely. He'd give his eye teeth for a hot shower and a cold martini.

Jack made a sorry sight. His once smart khaki bush-jacket, (Harrod's best, no expense spared) was torn and stained, his ginger hair was matted with sweat and every exposed surface of his city-pale skin was mottled and swollen by insect bites. To add insult to injury he hadn't got a single line on paper. He could feel the remains of his shaky career rapidly disappearing down the tubes. He shivered in the heat. All he needed was one lousy scoop. More chance of being struck by lightning in this neck of the woods.

He looked up at the darkening sky and crossed his fingers. No sense in tempting providence.

'Sorry Senor, eet ees 'opeless.'

Paco had given up and stood now, beside the ageing hack, fingering a crumpled map. 'We have to make camp here I think.

Too late to get back to the city before dark.'

'Here?' Jack's voice rose in alarm. 'What about the snakes and things?'

'There's one other possibilitee,' suggested his companion. 'We pretty close to the river. I no know if the mapa is good but looks like a small trading post mark here on the bank close by. Maybe we find a boat to take us down river or somebody help push the car out manana?'

Jack picked a leech off his leg and flung it from him with a shudder.

'What are we waiting for?' he said. 'Anything's better than sitting here listening to the frogs fart.'

Paco went to the car, returning with two rifles, one of which he handed to the reluctant reporter.

'Better take this Senor,' he said. 'In case we meet any alligators on the way.'

It was dusk when the two soldiers came out of the jungle and straggled up the overgrown path towards the bar. Pepita knew they were soldiers because of the colour of their clothes. Also they carried guns.

She had only seen soldiers once, when she was a child, but it was not a thing she would easily forget. A young warrior of her mother's tribe had made the mistake of killing and eating a white-man. The soldiers had come in the night. They had beaten the men and lain with the woman. They had laughed a lot, she remembered, loud laughter, with no pleasure in it.

Then they had taken the warrior away in chains.

To hang him.

They had not even done him the honour of allowing him to fight for his life like a human being.

It was the white man's justice, they said.

Many years had passed, years when Pepita had encountered much, good and bad. But the sight of those uniforms approaching through the half-dark sent a long-dormant ripple of apprehension whispering down her spine.

She spat, wondering what the soldiers were doing so far from the city. None of her business. Anyway she could use the custom. And what was there to be afraid of after all? They were only men.

Placing her hands on her ample haunches she put on her best smile and shouted loudly over her shoulder.

'Eh, Gordo. Set up los vasos. We got company.'

Jack Mack was not a tall man, but even he had to bend his head to get through the doorway. In doing so he almost came in contact with the native woman. God, she stank. The whole place stank.

In the warm, womb-like interior of the building, an obese figure stood behind the beer-stained bar, polishing glasses. Jack had never seen anyone so fat or so repulsive. He made the late Marlon Brando look as though he'd been attending Weight Watchers. Jack felt the hairs on the back of his neck start to rise. This could be his scoop?

'Fattest man in the world discovered in jungle', he thought. Not great but not bad.

Jack did what he always did when he could feel a story coming on. He started to whistle "Blue Suede Shoes".

The fat man's face wobbled and for one terrible moment Jack thought he was going to blub. Instead he began to back away, taking tiny, shuffling steps and making a sort of mewling sound, like a kitten in a drowning sack. When the wall precluded further retreat, he felt his way along to the corner of the room, pressing his overstuffed body against the wood as though trying to melt into the peeling paintwork.

Jack was not a sympathetic man. Nor was he made of stone. And clearly this bloke was in some distress. He moved towards the distraught figure, hands outstretched in friendship. 'Take it easy old son,' he said 'I'm a newspaper reporter and you're just the bloke I been looking for.'

The man made a noise, halfway between a snort and a laugh, and Jack's nostrils were suddenly assailed by an acrid whiff of long unwashed skin, overlaid by the unmistakable odor of pure terror. It almost took his breath away.

He had smelled it once in a cornered fox, when he was doing a piece on Royalty and blood-sports, but it was nothing as concentrated or overpowering as this.

He patted the plump shoulder in what he hoped was a reassuring manner.

'How would you like to be rich and famous?' he said.

For the fat man this seemed to be the last straw. The prospect was clearly too much for him. He gave a strangled gasp and his eyes turned up in their sockets revealing jaundiced whites. Then, as Jack bent towards him, a final paroxysm of horror shook the fat frame, the knees buckled and he fell with a crash like a collapsing mountain.

He twitched once and lay still.

Jack turned, his face ashen. New headlines formed before his eyes. "Newspaperman sentenced to death for murder of South American citizen".

Paco leant silently by the bar, looking ominous. No help there. Jack wished he'd been more friendly to the little crud.

In the gathering gloom the woman stood, outlined in the doorway, her face blank, her eyes veiled pools.

'He's... I think he's had some kind of a fit,' said Jack, who knew a heart attack when he saw one. 'I never touched him, honest I didn't. What's wrong with him?'

The woman said nothing. She merely moved to the fallen figure and, kneeling, raised the greasy head to cradle it in her lap.

The lids flickered open and unseeing eyes stared up into her face. Slowly the mouth stretched into a smile of seeming contentment.

'Momma,' the fat man said... and died.

Pepita stood looking down on the shallow grave, the stick of charcoal clutched in her hand. The soldiers had not stayed to help and so she had had to bury the man herself. It had not been easy but she had finally laid him to rest alongside her dead husband and the child whom she had put out of its misery.

The strangers had gone, back to their truck, to their barracks, to the outside world. They hadn't even waited for a beer.

El Capitan had seemed very upset by the fat man's death. He had even given her money, so that if anybody came, she would not tell.

What was to tell?

For some reason el Gordo thought they had come for him. That much she knew. He had been waiting many years for just such a visit. If the soldiers did not share her knowledge she was not about to tell them. She would not deliver his corpse up to the white man's justice. Whatever he had done, he had paid for with his life. And with the dreams that had terrorised him all these years.

Pepita felt that was enough. He had paid his dues. He was at peace now.

And so, when they asked her what he was called, she had said she didn't know.

'To me has always been "el Gordo",' she had said. 'The fat one.'

Now, standing by the grave she thought back, to that time, long ago, when he had told her his name.

It was soon after he had arrived. It was his cumpleanos... his birthday... and he had got very drunk. He told her many things then. How once in his own country he had been a great man. A Jefe. A Leader. A God almost. Worshipped by everyone. But in the end he hadn't been able to stand it anymore. The pressure. No privacy. Drugs to stay awake. Drugs to go to sleep. Like an animal in a cage. No life. So he had pretended to be dead. Had paid people to keep his secret. He had had plenty of money, he said, in the bad old days.

And then, next day, frightened and hung-over, he had begged her to forget it all.

She hadn't believed him anyway, had taken it for a drunkard's boasting. But she had always remembered the name. An unusual name. Soft and flaccid, like the man himself.

She bent down and, with the charcoal, scratched out the letters el Gordo had so painstakingly written in the dirt of the Cantina floor, all those years ago... EL   VIS.

History: This one was originally going to be about Hitler. But I changed my mind. It appeared in Fantasy Tales 7, *with a smashing illustration by Dave Carson. One in the eye for the paparazzi.*

CAT'S CRADLE

BASTIT LIES BY the fireside, sleek as midnight, dark as silk. Claws retracted, slitted eyes reflecting flame-light, measuring each movement as Matriarch instructs Granddaughter in the timeless intricacies of the Great Game.

Bone thin digits, deft with practice, weaving and interweaving secrets complex as womankind, inevitable as the season's changing. In and out, tight and loose, warp and weft, yin and yang until, with a final flick of the fingers, the corded tapestry becomes once more a single, quivering, fibrous strand.

How long is a piece of string?

As long as the line on the heart monitor when the pulse ceases and the soul spins spiralling into the void.

'Now you try.'

Grandmother loops cord-ends round childish index fingers. Clea, firstborn, hope for the future, carrying aloft the torch of feminine intuition, tied by a silver blood-cord to all those who have gone before, bends her auburn head over the puzzle, fierce in her concentration.

Sixty years since the Crone has sat just so, at her own Grand-mother's knee, absorbing the ancient truths inherent in the ageless, age-old patterns.

Another time, another place. Plus ça change, plus c'est la même chose.

Bastit runs a pink tongue over pointed teeth, arches her back, sphinx-like. She had had high hopes of that Grandmother-Child. Putative Sorceress in the making. But it was not to be. The latent promise, the magic eye, the universal overview dulled too soon by chores and mental arithmetic and an early marriage to a blinkered man whose small cruelties withered the Triple Goddess within. His reign had been brief. Bastit had seen to that, darting strategically between beer-fuddled legs as he crossed the Saturday night road, splaying him under the wheels of a passing pantechnicon.

But it was already too late. Virgin had become Mother, the Godhead ruptured, the subsequent girl-child born giftless. Her father's daughter, with no concept of her power or of the proper metaphysical scheme of things. The Game was beyond her. She had never managed to twist her fingers round the string, twisted them instead round a Company Director with a good job and a bad mistress in The City. No more than she deserved. No less. Birthright sold for a mess of pottage and a nice house in Highgate. An empty vessel. A vacant lot. Awash with all the worst aspects of the female gender. Petty, vain, shallow, selfish and spiteful. Her only claim to fame the child now sitting on the mat. A child who, at three, already knows more than her mother will ever comprehend.

Bastit casts an approving eye over pudgy, pearl tipped fingers computing the cosmic conjunctions as though the nail's sheen carries a reflection of the moon's phases. The power is strong in Clea, the Multi-Dimensional Memory absolute. In her baby hands she holds the secrets of the tides, the soul's mysteries. Flood, hurricane, earthquake and eruption ebb and flow as the small fingers fly, creating and un-creating reality.

Clea, controlling the life-force with a natural ability that comes maybe once in a thousand generations, harnessing her strength, preparing to redress the balance...

When did the pendulum swing? When did the usurper, that dealer in destruction, transplant the life-giver and plunge the world into darkness?

Bastit can remember a time when the death of a beloved cat caused the owner to shave off eyebrows in respectful mourning. What corrupt exercise in public relations turned the Demi-Goddess of Egypt into the loathed familiar, burned, flayed, tortured and torn asunder by order of some malignant Witchfinder General?

Now there is light at the end of the tunnel. Clea has power enough to break the entopic cycle, bring back the true Holy Trinity. Virgin, Mother, Crone. Gaia in all her guises. Love in all its phases. Unconditional, nurturing, compassionate.

If the new sibling doesn't stop her.

'Over my dead body', thinks Bastit, Cheshire smiling in secret knowledge of the several lives left her. Still, she will need all her feline cunning to succeed... to survive. Long gone are the days when killing one of her kind carried the death penalty. She must tread warily. And bide her time.

Rising languidly, tail poker straight, she stalks across the faded Persian rug, old almost as herself, and leaps lightly into Grandmother's lap.

As Crone runs an age-spotted hand over the smooth pelt, Bastit pushes her head back into the wrinkled palm and begins to purr. The sound swells to fill the enclosed space, pulsing against the twilight walls, thrumming deliciously in the blood, rhythmic and sensuous as the music of the spheres.

INTERIOR: TOWN HOUSE: DUSK.

We are in the sitting room of a well-appointed modern dwelling in an affluent suburb of North London.

It is twilight, the chill Autumn air kept firmly at bay by long velvet drapes the colour of blood, which cover the mullioned windows. Bulging bookcases display unread tomes bound in tooled leather. Brass and crystal twinkle in the flame-light of the fake log fire.

To the left of the marble fireplace stands an overstuffed armchair in which sits an elderly WOMAN with grey hair and a matching cardigan. A large brown CAT with bright green eyes lies in her lap. At her feet a small GIRL with a halo of red-blonde curls, plays Cat's Cradle with a piece of grubby string.

The noise of a car-horn breaks the silence. It is followed by sounds of banging doors and raised voices from off-stage.

Enter the HAPPY COUPLE, he beaming like a jackass, she clutching a small, swathed bundle to her Burberried bosom. A face, wrinkled as a walnut, purple as a prune, peers from amongst the crocheted shawl-folds. The eyes, berry bright as currants in a suet pudding, reflect the debauchery of many ages... and something else... a mixture of avarice and glee.

It is a face only a mother could love.

FATHER. Well, well. Here we are then. Safe and sound. The latest edition. The son and heir. Yes. Yes. Yes.

The little GIRL runs to her FATHER, wrapping herself round his knife-pleated trousers. He pats her shining head as one would a puppy.

MOTHER. (the sharp edge of jealousy in her voice). Clea. Leave Daddy alone. Don't you want to see your new brother?

CLEA steps back, face set, hesitant.

Her GRANDMOTHER rescues the awkward moment, rising to shuck the CAT from her lap, crossing from the fireplace, gathering CLEA to her en route and shepherding the child towards MOTHER and SON. Together they examine the new family member.

GRANDMOTHER. He looks like you, Joseph. (Clearly she does not mean this as a compliment).

FATHER, (oblivious to the irony, swelling like a pouter pigeon). Just what I said. My father's nose. We expect great things of him, eh Maria? Captain of Industry. Admiral of the Fleet. Maybe even PM?

MOTHER. Yes, darling. Whatever you say.

She goggles at the BABY, making small mewling sounds at him. He begins to cry. She looks round helplessly.

FATHER, (stepping back in case she should expect him to take delivery of the infant). Well, well. Must be off. Work to be done. No rest for the wicked.

MOTHER, (raising her thin voice to make herself heard over the baby's caterwauling). Oh, must you, Joseph? Not tonight, surely?

FATHER. Wish I didn't have to, of course. But duty calls. Another mouth to feed and all that. (He pats his wife's head, much as he has done his daughter's and pecks her absently on the cheek). Don't wait up. Bye Ma-in-law. Bye Clea.

He EXITS to the sound of his SON'S screaming.

Bastit trots into the hall, following the enemy to the triple-locked door. In Rome, where she'd been Guardian of the Household, there had been no need of such precautions. Open hearths. Everyone welcome. Barbarians excepted.

She insinuates herself against the dark worsted, feeling the leg within. Beneath the skin and bone, muscle and sinew, she senses the dark deceptions, the desire to be gone. Not to the phallic temple of the great God Mammon, tower thrusting into the City sky, but to the honeyed thighs of the current Jezebel, an overblown blonde awaiting his fevered gropings at a five star hotel across the Heath. Mr. and Mrs. Smith—no luggage. Booked in between Office and Hospital. A handsome pay-off to the smirking Concierge. Miss Jones from accounts, fresh from the shower, warm pink flesh bulging from the black negligee, slightly tiddley on the champagne sent up on the room tab, twirling the glass in fingers that will soon be caressing another, more pliant stem. Wriggling in delicious anticipation on the ample, king-size bed, watching adult movies on the in-house video. All part of the service.

A well-shone toe-cap catches Bastit in the ribs.

'Move it, Moggie.'

No need for pretence here in this darkened hallway. Each recognises the other for what they are. The key turns in the lock and he is gone in a swirl of aftershave and a slamming door.

Bastit lands in a ball of malice, hackles raised, memories of him—or one like him—walling her up alive in a Masonic foundation. Hoping to catch some of her magic. Distil it into the building's future. For good luck. Too blind to see that such mindless cruelty unleashes a back-lash. Cause and effect. Revenge is sweet, Bastit thinks. And near.

Regally, she stalks back into the drawing room, brushes accidentally against mother's stockinged leg, shudders at the pain seeping though the silk, tries to block it out, detach, fails, allows the shameful whining stream of consciousness to wash over her as it circles and re-circles in an endless wallowing loop of self-pity.

'Don't go, don't go, don't go. Don't leave me here, tonight of all nights. Haven't I been a good wife? Haven't I put you above all else, done all you wanted? Been your slave, your concubine? Given you a son? If only you knew the pain of the process—the agony—the tearing and rending, the splitting and cutting and sewing. The humiliation. The indignity. If men had babies somebody would have invented something more appropriate by now. What more can I do? What do you want from me? How can you leave me, tonight of all nights? You think I don't know where you're going, where you always go? Aren't I enough for you? Haven't I debased myself, done things I shudder to think of, filthy things it makes me sick to remember? And still you run off to your floozies with their big tits and their bigger appetites. And I'm left here with my po-faced mother and a three year old who should have been in bed hours ago and a smaller version of you. Little bastard. I wish he'd never been born. No, I don't mean that. Joseph... don't go, don't go, don't go. I need you. Joseph. Please come back.

INT: DRAWING ROOM: EVENING.

MOTHER, near to tears, hands SON to GRANDMOTHER.
MOTHER, Hold him, will you? I must have a gin.
GRANDMOTHER purses her mouth into small pleats of disapproval, returns to the inglenook and settles herself in the armchair, rocking the child, humming a snatch of lullaby.
GRANDMOTHER. He's wet.
MOTHER, (pouring herself a large one). Change him, there's a dear. You were always so much better at this stuff than me.
She nudges the padded bag perfunctorily towards the fireplace, adds ice to the glass, kicks off her shoes and sinks onto the sofa.
GRANDMOTHER sighs resignedly, unfolding the shawl and unpopping the babygrow.
GRANDMOTHER. Clea. Bring Grandma a nappy, there's a good girl. And the baby wipes and the zinc ointment.
CLEA does as she's bid, delving in the cavernous hold-all and delivering the items one at a time while her GRANDMOTHER

discards the sodden nappy and her MOTHER lays into the booze.

CLEA. What's that, Grandma?

CLEA, curious, stares at the small shrivelled scrotum, the tiny purpled glans.

GRANDMOTHER, (smothering the offending item in glook). That's what makes him a man, dear.

MOTHER. The source of all our sorrows. (She stands and moves unsteadily to the sideboard). I need a top up.

Bastit places a soft paw on the small, distended stomach and the baby stops crying, turning bland raisin eyes to stare, to threaten.

A red hot currant of energy jolts her psyche, almost causing her to withdraw. But she hangs on in there, forcing concentration, feeling the future form and flow across her inner eye. Bad enough her own fate at this monster's hands, hung from a tree, stomach slit, urinated on by a gang of screaming youths. This could be endured. Not so the death of countless hordes of innocent souls. In this child lies a quickening, a gathering of all things evil. The combined atrocities of Attila the Hun and Torquemada, Adolf Hitler and Vlad the Impaler will be as nothing compared to the outrages yet to be perpetrated by this seemingly innocent scrap of humanity. This helpless maggot. This small, smelly grub. Bastit knows only too well the metamorphosis these parasites can affect, bodies swelling, becoming more powerful, more dangerous, biding their time under the guise of harmlessness until the foulness is ready to burst through the cocoon, unleashing the cankerous butterfly within.

Clea is strong, but her strength, still unformed, will be stillborn in the face of this child's wickedness. The light of the world, snuffed out yet again.

Unless Bastit interferes.

As if to stiffen her resolve, the catalogue of horrors winds on. Cities reduced to rubble. Death and disease and wanton destruction. Plague and pestilence and putrid flesh stacked heaven-high. Sore-raddled children, skeletal in starvation, crying for mothers who lie violated in gutters running with blood.

A smell of juniper berries and embalming fluid penetrates the waking vision. Blood-tipped hands grasp Bastit's body, fling her up and away from the Apocalyptic Beast. Fur spiked in distaste, she skitters beneath the table, hissing out her hate.

INT: DRAWING ROOM: NIGHT.

CLEA. Don't do that to pussy. It's naughty.

MOTHER, (smacking the child across the head). Don't you speak to me like that, you little madam. Your precious daddy's not here to protect you now.

CLEA bursts into tears, runs to hide under the table, gathering the CAT into her arms, sobbing into the fur.

GRANDMOTHER. Maria. What's got into you? How dare you strike the child?

MOTHER. Spare me the lecture, you old harridan. How dare YOU let that smelly animal touch my son?

GRANDMOTHER. She wasn't doing any harm.

MOTHER. Filthy, dirty creature. Everyone knows cats carry disease. It could give him worms. It could give him flu. It could give him AIDS.

She snatches the BABY from GRANDMOTHER'S arms, balances him on her well-padded hip.

GRANDMOTHER, (standing). Nonsense. You're being hysterical. It's the hormones.

MOTHER. It's nothing to do with the hormones. Why, whenever I disagree with you is it always the hormones? Ever since I started the curse it's always been the goddamn hormones. Aren't I allowed a mind of my own? Can't I hate cats if I want to? Bloody animals. You always loved your cats more than me.

GRANDMOTHER, (laying her hands on her daughter's shoulders, trying to placate her). Maria, you're tired, darling. Otherwise you wouldn't be saying these things. You know perfectly well they're not true.

MOTHER. They ARE true. I should never have let Clea have that kitten. I knew no good would come of it. Nasty, scratchy thing. Well, that's all going to change. Tomorrow, first thing, it's going out. Out into the street.

Beneath the table, CLEA begins to howl louder, clutching the CAT to her chest, as though her life depended on it.

MOTHER, (ctd). For God's sake, Clea, stop that racket. I can't stand it. Go to your bed, right now.

GRANDMOTHER. Get a grip on yourself, Maria. You're frightening her.

She moves to the table to coax CLEA out from under it.

GRANDMOTHER, (ctd). Come to Grandma, darling. Mummy's tired. She doesn't mean it. Let's you and me and pussy go up to your room. I'll read you a bedtime story.

MOTHER. Not the cat. The cat stays here.

GRANDMOTHER. Whatever you say.

She gathers the little GIRL into her arms and exits left.

MOTHER places SON precariously on the sofa and totters over to pour herself another large gin.

The CAT hunkers beneath the table, antennae on pointed ear-tips quivering with static from the BABY'S silent laughter.

So it begins.

While MOTHER'S back is turned, the CAT slithers from its hiding-place and slinks out of the room.

MOTHER returns to the sofa, glass in hand. With difficulty, she unbuttons her blouse, produces a swollen breast and scoops her newborn SON into one crooked elbow. The BABY clamps on to the proffered nipple, begins to guzzle greedily.

GRANDMOTHER re-enters.

GRANDMOTHER. She's asleep. Went straight over.

MOTHER. She should have been in bed an hour ago. You spoil her.

She takes a large swallow of gin.

GRANDMOTHER. It was a special occasion. She wanted to see the baby.

MOTHER, (sourly). Wanted to see her daddy, more like.

GRANDMOTHER. I don't understand you, Maria. How can you be jealous of your own daughter? It's not healthy. It's only natural the child should be attached to her father.

MOTHER. Is it? I wouldn't know. I hardly knew mine. Maybe if you'd married again...

GRANDMOTHER. You were all I ever wanted. You... and now Clea.

MOTHER. Spare me the woman's sufficiency bit. It won't wash. You and Clea aren't anything like enough for me. I want more. Much more.

GRANDMOTHER, (gently). Just what DO you want, Maria?

MOTHER. Happiness. Security. A bit of attention once in a while.

GRANDMOTHER, (attempting to take the empty glass from her DAUGHTER'S hand). You won't find them in here.

MOTHER, (screaming). Don't preach at me. I'm not a child any more.

GRANDMOTHER. Then why are you behaving like one? (She leans across her daughter and holds out her arms). Give me the baby.

MOTHER clutches the BABY tightly, almost suffocating him.

MOTHER. Not this one. This one is mine. Clea always loved you more than me, but you're not having my son. Get out. Get out. You... you... baby-snatcher. Get out of my house.

GRANDMOTHER. Maria. You don't know what you're saying. You're drunk. Give me the baby before you do him some damage.

MOTHER. Get out. Are you deaf? Get out, I said. Leave. Vamoose. Bugger off.

She flings the glass across the room, the action dislodging the BABY from her nipple. The glass shatters in the fireplace. The BABY begins to bawl.

GRANDMOTHER, (stiffly). I'll get my coat.

Bastit sits in the bedroom window, gazing out at the night sky, washing the dust of the day from behind her elegant ears,

Behind her, Clea breathes quietly beneath the star-spangled duvet, sleeping the sleep of the just.

Below, in the rain-sodden street, the Crone steps from the front door and into the waiting taxi, pausing only to look up at her granddaughter's window, raising a hand in farewell to the Guardian at time's gate. A look of understanding passes between them. Then she is gone, into the infinity of the blue, black midnight, disappearing in a comet's trail of receding tail-lights.

Downstairs in the lounge, Mother mutters maudlin endearments to the thing she supposes is her son. Soon she will stagger to the nursery, deposit the cuckoo in its crib, before collapsing in her drunken stupor onto the loveless double bed next door, waiting in vain for her errant husband to creep home at dawn-light replete from his nocturnal callisthenics.

Then the house will be quiet.

All Bastit has to do is wait. She has waited for an eternity. She can wait a few minutes more.

Eventually Mother's footsteps echo on the stair.

Clea stirs at the sound, arms emerging from beneath the covers, fingers moulding the dreamscape. Poised between sleep and waking, cradled in the lap of infinity, she grasps the unseen umbilical cord of creation and begins to weave the best of all possible tomorrows.

Bastit awaits the signal of Mother's snoring. Then she rises and pads to the nursery, springing lightly into the crib. Slit-pupilled, she studies the tiny wizened features, the screw-shut eyes, the soft pulsing centre of the as yet unjoined skull bones. Gently, she settles herself over the button nose, blocking out the air, smothering the foulness once and for all. The thing stirs under her soft stomach.

Too late.

How long is a piece of string?

As long as the line on the heart monitor when the pulse ceases, the soul sinks screaming back into the abyss.

History: I was invited to submit something for an anthology about "Cats". I fear the editors may have been looking for something a little more "fluffy".

Whatever, they didn't take it. But I've always liked this story and offer it now as the only original piece in the collection. Enjoy.

BON APPETITE

IT WAS THE first time Fred and Martha had taken an off-base holiday and it had been somewhat less than successful. The Hire Rocket broke down continually, the weather stank and to cap it all, young Fred Jr, who was teething, yowled from morning till night.

On their last day, their so-called transportation packed up completely. With nothing else to do, they wandered into the maze of back-alleys that criss-crossed Celphi's capital city. In the lee of a crowded street market they came upon a small restaurant. On the shuttered front, in the forty known languages of the galaxy, a single-line message had been painstakingly scrawled. The English version ran as follows.

WE KATER FOR ALL TAYSTES - PLEEZE KOM INSIYD.

Martha raised her voice above Fred Jr's howling.

'Gee hon,' she screeched. 'I'm about starved. Ken we go in? They gotta sign in English. Maybe we ken getta decent meal forra change.'

'Some hopes,' snorted Fred. 'We haven't had a bite worth swallering since we landed on this Godforsaken planet. That goddam Travel Agent sure saw us coming. I ain't gonna fergit this holiday inna long time... Tarnashun's sake, Martha, don't that goddam kid EVER shut up'?'

The interior of the restaurant was dimly lit by a faint, pink glow. Its padded alcoves were furnished with low, silver tables and soft piles of embroidered cushions. As Fred and Martha entered, all heads swivelled in their direction. The ensuing silence was filled by the sound of Fred Jr, shrieking at the top of his voice.

A long, thin individual unwound himself from a corner and shimmied over. Like most of the customers he was bright purple in hue, had three legs, webbed fingers and a single large green eye. Murmuring in the soft guttural tones of the native Celphiian, he flapped his small, scaly wings in the traditional greeting.

'Gotta table?' Fred enquired loudly, clamping a sweaty hand over his son's squalling mouth. 'We want eat. You unnerstand?'

He pointed in the direction of his oesophagus and raised his voice another decibel. 'Eat. Savvy?'

The waiter beamed obligingly and ushered them to a vacant alcove.

'Goddam place is fulla geeks,' muttered Fred, lowering his flabby body onto the soft cushions. His wife plonked her skinny frame down beside him. Fred Jr, who was just dropping off to sleep, woke with a start and began exercising his lungs again.

'Dear Gawd, Martha,' yelled Fred. 'If you don't keep that goddam child quiet I'll go beeserk. I swear he hasn't closed his goddam trap in bleems. Well?' he shouted at the waiter who was standing expectantly at his left elbow. 'What're you waiting fer, dummy? Where's the goddam menu? Menu?' He used two podgy fingers to draw a square in the air, then pointed to his open mouth. 'MENU,' he roared. 'We want eat.'

The waiter smiled a purple smile and, producing a cube of plastic from a flap in his domed forehead, handed it to Fred with a flourish.

'Goddam forriners,' muttered Fred in disgust, turning the cube over and over in a vain attempt to decipher the Celphiian script. 'This ain't no good. Goddam geek language. Aintcha gotta English menu?'

The waiter raised his eyebrow.

'Holy Moses,' hollered Fred. 'What'm I doin here? I swear I'm like t'go crazy. This fool doesn't unnerstand a goddam word I say and I can't hear myself think fer the noise of that goddam baby. Here...' He thrust Fred Jr into the waiter's webbed hands. 'Put him somewheres til we've eaten. Somewheres I can't hear him. And bring us some chow. Anything.'

He made shooing motions at his screaming son and pointed at his mouth again for good measure.

The waiter bobbed his cyclopean head and undulated off.

The food, when it arrived, was a pleasant surprise. The vegetables were cooked to perfection and the meat fairly melted in the mouth. Fred and Martha stuffed themselves until every last morsel had gone. Then, sucking the remaining vestiges of gravy off his double chin, Fred gave a resounding belch and called for the bill and the baby.

When neither was forthcoming, he called for the Manager.

The Manager flapped his wings suavely and enquired, in impeccable English, whether the lady and gentleman had enjoyed their lunch?

'Never mind the goddam lunch. What we want now is the goddam baby,' Fred said, heatedly. 'Wheel it out. We gotta go.'

The Manager stretched his green eye wide. 'The baby, sir?' he said.

'Yeah, shouted Fred. 'Goddam it, the only one as speaks English is deaf. The BABY. And make it snappy.'

'Oh dear,' said the Manager. 'It would appear the waiter got the order wrong.' He wiggled his purple ears in apology. 'The baby... er... I'm afraid there's been a dreadful mistake...

History: Originally set in a Chinese restaurant and involving a Pekinese, this is another variation on an old joke theme. I just had to take it one stage further, didn't I? Written to be read on 'Moment of Terror' it also made it as a "tail ender"— again in Fantasy Tales. *Volume 8, Number 16 if memory serves.*

OVER MY DEAD BODY

A S JOSH APPEARED in the doorway, coffee-steaming cup to his lips, she noted that his body, so eminently desirable the night before, had that flaccid, fishbelly pallor that spoke of sheltered winters spent in stuffy rooms. She covered her eyes in protest as he flung the windows wide and tumbled her out of bed.

'I hate a man who's cheerful in the morning,' she seethed, scrabbling through the layers of her unpacked suitcase. 'Oh Christ. Don't tell me I've forgotten my bikini. That's all I need.'

Josh roared with laughter, throwing his head back and bellowing like a bull. She winced, cradling her hangover in protective hands as he grabbed her shoulders and steered her to the window.

The empty sand, bleached as a pirate's bones, stretched unbroken from the villa to the water's edge. Nothing stirred.

'Observe,' said Josh. 'We are alone. No prying eyes. No nosy neighbours. No peeping Toms. Bikinis are as superfluous here as the proverbial coals in Newcastle.' He flung her, still protesting, over his shoulder and carried her out into the sunstreaked morning. Stumbling over soft sand to the sea, he waded in thigh deep before hurling her, kicking and screaming, into the water.

The shock of it startled her awake and scattered the remnants of her bad temper. They dived and fought, wrestling around in the shallows in mock ferocity until, sides aching from the unaccustomed exercise, they dragged themselves out and flopped onto the warm sand.

Josh leaned over her, the sun prisming the droplets of water on his greying hair into a silver halo. Consumed by a sudden rush of tenderness, she sat up and kissed him.

'Don't move,' he ordered. 'You are about to discover yet another of my many talents. Stay here and get some sun. I'll call you when breakfast's ready.'

She rolled over on her stomach using her interlinked hands to appropriated her alter ego.

Accident or design?

Need she even ask?

Nothing Meredith did was ever unpremeditated. Gareth must have given the game away and her rival, knowing how much better she would look in black, had deliberately decided to upstage her on her own territory.

Good thinking, girl wonder, because in this instance comparisons were odious indeed. Where the funereal gown consumed what little colour Olwyn had, hanging like a rag on her sparrow thin frame, Meredith's voluptuous figure moulded the material into a couture creation. Her face, conker brown from a recent trip to Lanzarote, positively glowed with good health as she removed the mask to kiss the Prince of Darkness lingeringly on the lips, Gareth repaying the compliment with interest.

'Besotted,' Olwyn thought, oscillating between resignation and hysteria. 'Bewitched. While all my sorry spells are turned to dust.'

Under cover of the ensuing guffaws and greetings, she stumbled down the remaining stairs and slunk, unnoticed, into the kitchen.

'Don't be a victim...' Her erstwhile friends. Easy for them to say.

It had happened so gradually. Like some wasting disease. She had gladly given her life over to Gareth's happiness. Protected, nurtured, cherished him. When they discovered there would be no children (his fault, not hers), she had never once uttered a word of reproach, instead subsuming all her maternal instincts into his welfare. Waiting to greet him when he returned from class, slippers ready, dinner on the table. She, who had got the better grades, melting into the background so that he might shine. Dressing discretely so as not to embarrass him. Never voicing an opinion that might contradict his. Content in her role of power behind the throne.

'That's why you'll always find me in the kitchen at parties,' she hummed a snatch of a tune from their hey-days, when she'd still been the belle of the ball, sloshing a monumental wallop of scotch into a beer mug, swallowing it neat.

So now he'd fallen in love with a woman who represented everything he had always purported to despise. A big, brassy, blonde divorcee with two teenage children and an eye to the main chance.

'Witchcraft,' she muttered to herself. It was the only logical explanation.

Another large measure of the hard stuff screwed up her courage enough for Olwyn to totter into the drawing room and begin to mingle. She might as well not have bothered. No one paid her the slightest bit of attention or even acknowledged her presence. She attached herself to group after group, trying her best to look interested, or as interested as one CAN look with a face like Punch and a wart on the end of one's nose. She hovered pathetically on the periphery of conversations but not a single person drew her into the circle or encouraged her to chat.

She was yesterday's news. Persona non grata in her own house. Last season's fashion. A has-been. A no-hoper. A dead duck.

Across the room, her identical twin held court in the centre of an adulatory male circle. Meredith la Fé. Sex Goddess. Husband hunter. Queen of the night. Spinning her web to entrap the unwary.

The eyes, sly and knowing, taunted from behind the mask, gloating at her rival's discomfort, and Olwyn's imagination was suddenly beset by a premonition of poor Gareth sucked dry as a husk, discarded amongst a pile of what had once been other men, other lives.

'I see you for what you are,' she thought, and Meredith's eyes replied... 'But what good will it do you?' while her mouth cried... 'Come on you handsome Devil, let's have a dance,' and then, insultingly, as though she hadn't seen her, 'When's Olwyn coming down?'

'Shortly,' he said, eyes only for his mistress. 'Having one of her headaches,' and they waltzed out into the hall, leaving the other guests to nudge each other and wink knowingly and carry on with their gossip.

Devastated, humiliated beyond measure, Olwyn rushed back

make a cushion for her head. She was as completely happy as she could remember being for a long time. Relaxed and at peace, she dropped into a contented doze.

When his call came, she opened her eyes, peering through the tangled curtain of her hair along the white expanse of lonely beach. Through the rising heat-haze she saw a figure moving across the sand towards her. She sat up hastily, aware of her nudity, and tried to cover herself as best she could with one hand, sweeping the hair back from her eyes with the other. But when she looked again, the figure had disappeared.

Shrugging the image away as a "trick of the light", she ran up the beach towards the tantalizing smell of freshly perked coffee.

The days melted into nights and back into days again. Now and then, sunbathing in a semi-stupor, she was conscious of the prickling sensation that comes with being observed. And several times she was sure she glimpsed the figure out of the corner of her eye. Of course when she put on her sunglasses for a proper look, there was nothing there. She was intrigued, nothing more. She didn't mention it to Josh for fear he might laugh at her.

It had been a glorious evening. After dinner they sat outside on the terrace drinking and talking until late, swathed in the tortuous make-believe of their love game.

Bed that night was particularly satisfying. Afterwards she lay in the crook of his arm, watching his dormant face, building each plane and angle into a picture-memory that would carry her through the imminent separation. It was her own fault that she'd got involved knowing that it could never lead anywhere. She always went for no-hopers. Story of her life.

Engrossed in self-analysis, trying to subdue the encroaching angst, at first she hardly noticed the small, scuffling sounds. When she did, she wasn't unduly alarmed, putting them down to some inquisitive night creature that had strayed from its usual haunts. Not until the noises became loud enough for her to distinguish them over the ebb and flow of the surf, did she realize that something was moving furtively around the house.

The tiny hairs rose off the back of her arms and her skin puckered into gooseflesh. Sitting up, she shook the sleeping body beside her

'Wha...Wharzamatter?'

'There's someone outside the window. I think they're trying to get in.'

They listened, ears straining.

Presently he sighed and said 'Well, there's nothing there now. Whatever it is or was, it's gone away.'

He pulled her to him, cradling her head against his shoulder.

'I thought it was that tall person I sometimes see on the beach.' she said in a small voice.

'What tall person? There hasn't been a soul here since we arrived.'

'There has too. He's Arabic I think. Wears a long, white robe.'

'You're letting your imagination run away with you, my dear. Probably a touch of the sun.'

She gritted her teeth. 'Don't patronize me. I HAVE seen someone on the beach. Maybe your wife's sent a spy to keep an eye on us?'

'Now you're being ridiculous. She hasn't the faintest notion I'm in Morocco. Only Jack knows and he won't tell. She thinks I'm in Hamburg at the Conference. She's always trusted me implicitly.'

'More fool her,' she said sarcastically. 'Anyway we made a pact not to talk about her while we were here?'

'You're the one who started it. You and your imaginary, skulking Arabs.'

Stung, she turned away from him. 'Go to sleep,' she said. 'Serve you right if we were murdered in our beds.'

Next morning the sky was overcast. Neither was willing to say "sorry" and what had been a trivial disagreement deepened as the day went on.

In the afternoon Josh went for a walk. Alone. With no sun, no radio and no newspapers, boredom rapidly overtook her and with it, regret for the high-handed attitude which had prompted her to stay behind. As soon as he came back she would apologize. With so little time left it was ridiculous to waste it bickering. She slipped on her sandals and went outside.

He was already halfway home, shoulders hunched, hands in pockets, staring at his feet as he walked. Her heart lurched in remorse.

She began to hurry towards him, then stopped. Behind him the tall, white-robed figure moved like a shadow in negative. In the time it took for her to raise her hand to shade her eyes, the figure had merged, like a mirage, into the surrounding sand and Josh was already running towards her. He flung his arms round her in a bear hug, squeezing the breath from her body like the juice from an orange.

'You're shivering,' he said in conciliatory tones. 'Come inside. What you need is a glass of wine and a nice cuddle.'

She looked nervously over her shoulder. But the beach was deserted. Gently, he led her towards sanctuary.

Her eyes shot open. For one hideous, disorientating moment, she couldn't remember where she was. Then, with the sound, memory flooded back.

Someone was moving round the house again. She could hear breathing this time, shallow and laboured. Whoever it was began to scrabble at the shutters. The breathing became louder, more painful, rasping in the prowler's throat. Then, to her horror, a hand crept through the shutters, groping blindly, fumbling for the catch.

She found her voice and with all the lung-power at her command, began to scream. The hand hastily withdrew. But that didn't stop her. Startled from sleep, brutal in his anxiety, Josh shook her until her teeth rattled. Still she screamed, eyes and mouth wide with terror. Finally he slapped her, twice, across the face. The screaming subsided into a low moan.

Josh strode to the window.

'Don't open it,' she screamed, cowering down in the bed. But he had already undone the faulty catch and flung the shutters wide.

Outside, the almost full moon hung serenely in an untroubled sky. Across the shutters, a spider trail of blood led to nowhere.

She was alone on the beach. Josh had driven to town to exchange their flight tickets for the earliest return places available. In the hard light of day his assurances that the blood had been the remains of an unusually large mosquito didn't seem so far-fetched.

But the night before she had begged and pleaded for him to take her home. The holiday was ruined. The anticipated magic of their clandestine fortnight's bliss had been blighted like a wheat-field in a drought.

She lay in the sun and reasoned with herself, trying to explain away the events of the previous evening. It was probably strain. Interdepartmental affairs were never easy things with which to cope. Keeping it from the "perfect wife" didn't help. A bitter woman with more money than sense, clinging to a man who didn't love her. Or so HE said.

'Life goes on,' she said, flopping into the water, immersing herself in the buoyant, green clearness of it. She did a brisk crawl for a hundred yards then rolled over on her back. The mid-afternoon heat-haze shimmered the outlines of the villa into iridescent eddies, merging stone into sand. The seawater massaged her limbs, the afternoon sun caressed her bobbing head. Gradually her melancholia dispersed. Refreshed, she began to breast-stroke lazily towards land.

She had almost reached the shore-line when she saw the figure. It stood outside the bedroom window, peering in. Her heart gave an almighty jolt and she sank, swallowing vast quantities of salt water. When she rose to the surface, coughing and spluttering, it had moved. Now it stood before the open door. It hesitated for a moment, then shuffled awkwardly inside.

In an instant, her fear evaporated and was replaced by an overwhelming, irrational rage. She half-swam, half-ploughed her way to shore, stumbled up the beach towards the villa and plunged furiously inside shouting as she went. The main room was empty. She flung open the bedroom door.

'There's no use hiding,' she yelled 'I know you're in there somewhere.'

She rushed into the bathroom, her voice shrilling in anger. 'What do you want with us? Why can't you leave us alone?'

Back in the bedroom she tore open cupboards, got down on her hands and knees to look under the bed, ripped out drawers. Yelling, cursing, crying with frustration. And that was how Josh found her when he returned from town, standing stark naked, hands on hips, in the centre of the main room, screaming her defiance to the empty air.

By the time they had tidied up the mess, the sun had set. She insisted that he repair the latch on the window shutters and double lock the door before she would go to bed.

There was no question of their making love. Presently, from the sound of his breathing, she realized that he had fallen asleep. He thought she was crazy. Off her rocker, was how he'd so charmingly put it. Her left arm had gone numb. She turned, tentatively, to ease the "pins and needles" and the bed creaked.

Or was it the bed?

Instantly she was wide awake. The progress round the house had begun. The breathing and shuffling sounds were noticeably louder than they had been on the two previous nights. Cold sweat broke out on her forehead.

The prowler stopped outside the window, scrabbled at the catch and discovering that it had been strengthened, moved on. It reached the front door. She listened, petrified, to the knob being turned this way and that.

Then suddenly, whatever it was lost control. It rattled the doorknob furiously and began to scratch and bang at the woodwork. Its laboured breathing turned to grunts of rage.

Beside her Josh stirred, woke, heard the din, sat up.

'You think I'm imagining things now?' she hissed through clenched teeth. 'Listen to it. It's going to break the door down soon.'

Josh swung his legs over the edge of the bed and marched purposefully into the other room. Her spine turned to jelly as she heard him draw back the bolts and swing open the door. A draught of stagnant, icy air swept into the room, stirring the sheets with its foetid breath.

There was a momentary pause. Then she heard him scream. The sound came out as a gurgling wail of disbelief.

Eventually even that stopped. She lay still, not daring to breathe. Five seconds passed. Ten. Fifteen. She sat up gingerly, looking around for some weapon with which to protect herself. Lifting the heavy ashtray from the bedside table she tip-toed shakily into the main room.

Josh lay crumpled on the floor, his ravaged features a Hallow-een mask of terror. Over him, backlit by the silvery glow of the full moon, crouched the figure in white.

Now that she was close enough to tell, she realized with a shock that it wasn't a man at all. It was a woman wearing a hospital gown stained with blood. It raised its head to look at her, the one good eye glinting with malice. In that horrifying moment of recognition, the ashtray plunged from her nerveless fingers to shatter on the tiled floor.

The figure placed one propriatorial hand on the body and drew back its lips in the hideous facsimile of a smile.

The messenger who arrived on his moped next morning found her catatonic in a corner, hair plastered to her head, vacant eyes staring at the naked body of her lover. The foreign gentleman had evidently died of a heart attack and she poor lady, would never speak again.

In his haste to alert the Police to the tragedy, the little man dropped the week-old telegram he had come to deliver. A tiny tornado of wind whipped it across the empty beach into the water where it floated, a snowflake on the swell, until the orb of the sun had bleached away the words which since he spoke no English, the Arab had failed to understand.

"Emily killed in car accident," it read. "Come home

immediately. Jack".

History: 'Over My Dead Body' was written to be included in a supplement of short stories attached to the bumper summer edition of a now sadly defunct magazine called Best. *Not exactly* The New Yorker *but with a not inconsiderable print run. There were half a dozen stories in all, designed to divert those holidaymakers taking a break from basking on the beach. Mine was the only one that didn't have a happy ending. Ho ho. It was later re-printed in the South African magazine* Keur.

CATCAWLS

On wild wintry evenings,
When stormclouds are whipped,
You might see a Catcawl
Creep out of a Crypt.
They live in the graveyard
Deep under the stones
In bloodcurdling caverns
Constructed from bones,
That eerily echo
With screeches and groans.
They huddle together
Deep under the rime
Where they munch mouldy marrow
And freshly chilled slime
And eyes—which they polish off
Four at a time.
Beware of the Catcawl
Who's frequently found
By gravediggers working
The freshly tilled ground.
Best to stay in your bed
Huddled under the sheets.
Catcawls stalk in the darkness
Patrolling the streets.
They hide around corners
Where runaways play
To trap the unwary
And steal them away.
'And how will I know them,'
I hear you enquire,
'These Catcawls with habits

So dreath and so dire?'
It's hard to mistake them
When once they've been seen.
Their noses are wormeaten,
Mouths are obscene
And their ears are like cabbage leaves
Wrinkled and green.
Their teeth are like razors
Stained bloodily red.
They have one eye, which sits
On the top of their head.
They're covered in hair.
They're disgustingly fat.
A kind of a cross
'Twixt a frog and a rat.
And their breath...
Well their breath has
The stench of the tomb
And their catcalling calls
Like the knelling of doom
As it gloats through the gloaming
And girns in the gloom.
They chuckle and chortle
And cackle in glee
At the prospect of meeting
With you or with me.
So it's best to stay in
When you've finished your tea.
For they prowl through the night-time
Like Vampires, like voles
And they're not altogether
The kindest of souls.
'But where do they come from,'
You want me to tell,
'These horrible freaks,
It must surely be Hell?'

Well I couldn't be certain,
It may not be true,
But I have heard it said,
Between me, between you,
That Catcawls are children
Who've been very bad
Who're rude to their elders
And drive their Mums mad
Who spit at the postman
Who walk on the grass
And stick out their feet
When old ladies go past.
Who don't do their homework
Who won't clean their teeth
And who lift up the carpet
To see what's beneath.
I've heard, though it may be
A tissue of lies,
That children who pinch
All the Christmas mince pies
Are turned into Catcawls
At dead of the night
And spirited off
Long before it is light
To those damp, hollow hutches
Deep under the ground
And kept there—
'Til two hundred years have turned round.
So if you've been wicked
You'd better watch out.
Make sure you behave
If a Catcawl's about.
For if this story's real,
Yes, suppose it's all *true*,
The next to creep out of the crypt
Could be *YOU!*

History: A poem rather than a short story, 'Catcawls' was commissioned by Neil Gaiman and Steve Jones for their phenomenally successful collection of nasty verse 'Now We Are Sick'. Blamed by the editors on Clive Barker, who did some of the original illustrations, not only has this little gem had English and American editions, in hard and paperback, but the anthology has been translated variously into French (Tous Malades, 2006), Greek (Apposthemena Myana, 2008) and Spanish (under its original name, but with the subtitle 'una antologia de versos espantosos', in 2011). The latter, published by "23 Escalones" (also publishers of my novel Amy) won the Spanish horror writers' Nocte Award for best foreign book in translation in 2012. Not bad since the original first saw the light of day twenty years previous in 1991 (with reprints in 1994 and 2005). Unique of its kind, it's a collector's item if ever there was one.

SEA CHANGE

H E OPENED HIS mouth to scream but the sound was stillborn, silenced by an inrush of salty water. He sank, struggling feebly, his flailing arms powerless against the churning weight that forced him down and down.

Like a broken toy the sea grasped him and thrust him to the surface again. He felt a momentary current of cold air against his face before he sank once more.

Time stopped, became a single, continuous, bone-crushing moment without beginning or end.

Consciousness receded.

And then she was there. Her sturdy arms were round him, holding him up, bringing him to the surface. To light and air. And life.

She swam strongly for a girl, one arm around his neck to keep his chin out of the water. She was hampered somewhat by her cumbersome clothing and the long, red hair which swept about her head like seawrack, clinging to her eyes and mouth. And all the way to shore the sea tugged at her angrily, loth to deliver up its prey having once ensnared it.

Her feet touched bottom and she stood up, holding the child to her tightly. She steadied herself on the uneven shingle then carried him up the beach and laid him tenderly on the sand. She rubbed his bloodless hands, chafing the nerveless fingers.

'Stephen, don't die on me,' she pleaded. 'Stephen. Speak to me. Are you living at all?' Her voice was gentle, coloured by the soft, west of Ireland brogue.

The boy opened his eyes.

Her smile was gentle too, lighting up the amber eyes like sunshine stealing from behind a cloud.

He tried to speak but gagged instead, seawater gushing from

his mouth. She lifted his head, propping it against her warm body, patting his back and murmuring to him in her lilting accent.

'There you are now allana. Rosheen is here. No need to fret my love. You're safe now. Safe and sound.'

The spasm ended. He looked up at her with frank curiosity, at her golden eyes, her buttermilk skin.

'How did you know my name was Stephen?'

'Ach, now and why shouldn't I know?' She turned, head cocked, listening. 'Whist,' she said. 'Someone's calling you.'

A man stumbled over the foreshore. Face gaunt with worry, he shouted into the wind. 'Stephen, where are you? Stephen!'

'It's my father,' said the boy.

'Of course,' the girl answered. 'And it would be.'

The man stopped, taking in the frozen tableau of the huddled boy and kneeling girl. Then he began to run towards them.

'I must go now,' the girl smiled.

'Why?' asked the child, dark eyes questioning.

'Just because I must,' she said and she stood and moved silently away through the sand-dunes.

'Stephen.' The man's voice was angry with relief. 'Where have you been? How many times have I told you not to come down to the beach without me? My God, you're soaked. What happened?'

'I fell in.' The boy looked at him solemnly. 'I was trying to catch a jelly-fish and then I fell in. The lady saved me. The lady with the red hair. She ran away.'

'I know. I saw her,' said his father, hunkering down. 'Come on, let's get you home before you catch your death of cold. Can you walk or do you want me to carry you?'

'Of course I can walk,' said the boy, stiffly. 'I'm not a baby.'

He trudged up the beach ahead of his father. The wind whipped his fine fair hair back from his forehead and danced around his small body, flattening the yellow mackintosh against his frail chest, bullying and buffeting him until he had to use all his strength to stay upright.

They walked some way in silence. Then the boy spoke, keeping his eyes glued to the ground.

'Her name's Rosheen,' he volunteered. 'And I'm sorry she went away.' He stopped, casually nudging a stone with the toe of his wellington. 'I think I'll probably marry her when I grow up.' He turned his gaze to the man beside him. 'She's very beautiful, isn't she father?'

The man thought of her, running like a startled faun through the sandhills, her strangely archaic dress clinging to her young body, wild russet hair flowing behind her in damp tendrils. A painting by Dante Gabriel Rossetti.

'Yes Stephen,' he agreed. 'Very beautiful.' He looked at the pounding sea and shuddered. 'And very brave to have saved you from that.' For once his natural reserve almost deserted him and he had to bite his lip to stop himself flinging his arms round his son and holding him close. To have lost the two of them, one after the other. Could he have coped with that? Then his upbringing re-established itself. The memory of his own father upbraiding him when fell over and cried. 'Real men don't show emotion. Richard'. The scorn in the harsh voice still rankled all these years on 'I must ask old O'Hara where she lives,' he said. 'Tomorrow we'll go and thank her.'

The boy slipped his small hand into his father's large one.

'Good,' he said. 'I'd like that.'

It was night. The storm howled with unabated ferocity round the thick, stone walls of the old inn, making the hurricane lamps flicker in the smoke-laden air. The rain had begun just after dark and now it pounded against the windows like a maniac screaming to come in.

In the ingle-nook before the dying turf fire the man sipped his hot toddy and gazed pensively into the smouldering embers.

'Is himself asleep, then?' Seamus O'Hara, proprietor of Derrymore's only hostelry bent over the fire and poked a spill into the glowing turves to light his pipe.

'Fast asleep thanks,' replied the man. 'He didn't even finish his cocoa.'

'Sure now and don't children have the marvellous powers of recovery?' said the old man, pausing between words to puff his battered clay pipe to life. 'It must have been a terrible shock to him at the time. And lucky escape he had, thanks be to God, but he'll have forgotten all about it in the morning.'

'I don't think so, though as you say, he doesn't seem to be upset at all. But he's very taken with the girl who rescued him. He won't have forgotten her. Wants to marry her, he says.'

'Bless us and save us, and aren't they young at the falling in love these days?' laughed the landlord. 'Which girl is this now? You didn't tell me any of this earlier on.'

'I don't know who she is. I thought you might tell me where she lives so that Stephen and I can go and thank her. I didn't speak to her myself. She ran away before I got the chance. But I'd know her again anywhere. She had the most amazing hair. Dark red. Copper coloured almost. Long and thick, like a horse's mane.'

Mr. O'Hara looked up sharply.

'Red hair, did you say? It didn't happen to strike you now did it, that her clothes looked a bit old-fashioned?'

'Now that you mention it, it did. You know her then?'

'There's not many in Derrymore as don't know Rosheen.'

'Rosheen. That's right. Stephen said her name was Rosheen. Perhaps you could take us to see her tomorrow?'

The landlord shivered even though the room was hot.

'I'll take *you* to see her tomorrow, Mr. Anderson,' he said, obliquely. 'After that you'll have to decide for yourself whether or not you want to take the boy.'

'What do you mean?'

'Sure I'll say no more about it for now. You'll be finding out soon enough.' He stood up and patted his guest on the shoulder. 'It a wild night, Mr. Anderson. Can I get you a last jar now before you go to bed?'

The wind sang softly through the dune-grass, an ageless, age-old song of love and death. The storm had blown itself out during the night and morning had dawned eggshell blue.

The two men tramped over the sandhills, threading their way between mounds of scutch grass and hummocks of drying carrigeen. They made an oddly contrasting couple, the one tall and straight in his city overcoat, the other enveloped in baggy tweeds that fitted where they touched.

'Was himself cross now, when you said he couldn't come?' asked the old man.

'No, not cross. He was disappointed but he didn't say much. Sometimes I wish he would make more fuss about things. He's been very quiet since his mother died. I worry about him.'

Embarrassed at having confided even this to a stranger, he changed the subject.

'I didn't realize there were any houses along the beach Mr. O'Hara.'

The old man stopped, hands in his pockets and tilted his seamed face to the sky. He sniffed appreciatively at the ozone-scented air.

'Isn't it the breath of Heaven that's in this morning?' he observed. Then, satisfied that his companion had got over his discomfort, he carried on as though he had never halted.

'No, you'll not find many houses, that's the truth,' he said, wryly. 'But it's a different type of dwelling we'll be visiting today. Preserve yourself in patience Mr. Anderson. We're nearly there.'

They topped the ridge of the next sand dune and the old man stopped, pointing down into the hollow.

This is it,' he said. 'This is Rosheen's home.'

Below them, almost hidden from sight by the windswept rises around it, a pathetic, overgrown mound pushed itself up from among the flotsam of ages. At one end stood a weathered headstone, tilted slightly to one side.

'I don't understand,' said Anderson.'

'Look at the inscription.'

Slithering and sliding down into the dip, the man bent over the unkempt grave and brushed away the sand so that he might read the name carved into the stone.

ROSHEEN FINNEGAN
BORN 1921 ~ DIED 1938

He straightened up. 'You're mistaken. It's impossible. I tell you I *saw* this girl.'

'Sure and haven't we all seen her at one time or another? Poor creature, she never rested easy. Especially when there was a storm about. Then she'd always be out here on the beach. Looking for the child. Calling his name.'

'But that's ridiculous. You're not going to tell me that my son was rescued by a ghost?'

'Och now I'm not in a position to tell a man like yourself anything, Mr. Anderson. Except maybe Rosheen's story. And that only second-hand, for wasn't I working across the water the time it happened? I had it from my father. If must be fifty years ago. Doesn't the time fly too?

'There was this couple from London. You're from London yourself aren't you Mr. Anderson?'

The visitor nodded impatiently.

'Well, anyway, this couple used to come here every year on their summer holidays. They came first on their honeymoon and liked it so much they came back every year after, first with their daughter and then with a young son. The last time they came they took on a girl to help with the children. She wasn't from these parts, she came from further west I think. She was hardly more than a child herself but by all accounts she was a powerful hand with the youngsters. Her name was Rosheen.

'The boy was mad keen on the fishing and nothing would do him but they should take a row-boat out in the bay. He tavered Rosheen's brain with it so much that at last, for a bit of head ease, she gave in to him. The upshot of it was that a freak storm blew up and the boat capsized. Rosheen managed to save the little girl but she herself was drowned trying to find the boy. Her body was swept up three days afterwards but the child was never recovered.

'They buried her on the beach. It's the custom you know, with drowned ones. And anyway, she hadn't had the sacraments so they couldn't put her in the cemetery.'

He looked down on the small untended grave.

'But she never rested God help her. The boy was her favourite. It's as though she couldn't forgive herself. Ach well. This might make it better. A life for a life. Now that she's saved your son maybe she'll lie easier?'

Anderson looked at the neglected hummock, remembering her gait, her youth, her hair.

'I hope she does,' he said feelingly. 'Though I still can't believe it.'

'Then far be it from me to try to persuade you,' the old man searched for words. 'I know a modern man like yourself will find an occurrence such as this difficult to understand. But there's many a thing I've seen here that defies normal explanation. Ireland's a beautiful country. But it's a strange one too. We seem to be closer to the mysteries here.'

The younger man looked startled.

'Do you know, Mr. O'Hara, that's just what my grandmother used to say.'

'Did she indeed?' the old man was clearly pleased. 'She's been to Ireland then has she?'

Anderson nodded.

'And did she ever get as far as Derrymore?'

'Indeed she did. When she was a child. She and the family came every summer on holiday... until...' he paused, suddenly aware of what he had said and what he was about to say... 'Until the accident. Her brother was drowned.

'I called my son after him. His name was Stephen too.'

History: Richard Davis included this story in his Spectre 4 *anthology, which was published in 1977. 1977 seems to have been particularly prolific for me. Richard also took another of my stories 'The Chosen' for* Space 4 *the same year. Both collections were aimed at young adults but I think 'Seachange' can't really be categorised. It aims to show that not all spectres rattle chains and scare one out of one's wits. Some are guardian angels in disguise.*

WHICH WITCH

'I LOOK LIKE death,' said Olwyn, smoothing one taloned finger across a shadowed eye socket.

Fishbelly skin. Bloodless lips.

Not a pretty sight.

She picked up the monstrous rubber mask, securing it under the black acrylic wig with an elastic band, peering through the eye-slits at her transmogrified features. Snow-white's wicked stepmother to the life... 'Mirror, mirror on the wall...'

To her left, in her parallax view, Gareth fiddled with the window catch, raising the sash to admit a small tornado of parched leaves, paper thin in their antiquity. They spiralled down to the carpet like dead dreams, shuddered once and lay still. In their wake, the dank October evening slithered across the sill, carried on the wings of a night wind spotted by rain.

Olwyn shivered, pulling the sombre satin smock closer to her ectomorphic frame, staring into the stained mercury of the Victorian looking glass as though, at any moment, she expected the hounds of hell to appear from its mirrored perspective, baying for her blood.

Enough of these fanciful notions. She had had too many of them lately. Omens in the tea-leaves. Presentiments of doom in the fall of an apple skin. She shook away the morbid fears, turning her gaze on her errant husband, chiding him in the glacial tones of the dispossessed.

'Would you mind closing the window? Anyone would think it was mid-summer rather than Halloween.'

But as so often lately, Gareth ignored her, striding from the room, face oddly flushed. Lips set in a thin line, slamming the door behind him.

A cold hand clutched at Olwyn's heart.

She turned back to her reflection, jamming the witch's hat on top of the gargoyle features. Behind the mask, her tired eyes brimmed with tears.

'Come, come,' she said, blinking them away. 'This will never do. Whatever will the neighbours think? Time to put on a brave face.'

She smiled and the mask smiled sardonically back. Ugly as sin. Olwyn got to her feet and, with a final over the shoulder glance at her reflection, left the room, switching off the light as she went.

Downstairs all was laughter and bustle, a world away from the graveyard damp outside the bedroom window. Olwyn stood looking over the carved banister, trying to pluck up enough courage to join the revels. Who were these people anyway? Gareth's cronies from the University. His friends. Not hers. She had given hers up when they'd got married. How many moons ago?

'Keep your options open,' they had advised, kindly. 'You're as clever as he is. Cleverer. Don't turn yourself into a doormat.'

And she, heedless, head-over-heels, had naturally ignored them all.

Goblins and Ghouls. Medieval Popes and Celtic Druids. Warlocks and Enchantresses. Skeletons and Vampires. Vaguely familiar faces in unfamiliar guise, crowded together in Bacchanalian bonhomie, while the sound system pounded out a latter day Dance of Death. The Stones – Devil Woman.

From her elevated viewpoint Olwyn felt suddenly, smugly superior. In the scene but not of it. Detached behind her frowsy rubber face.

What idiots they were really. What hypocritical buffoons. Why should she care what they thought? Did their ridiculous opinions matter when all was said and done? How dare they censure her for holding on to what was rightfully hers? Shaking their interfering heads, agreeing among themselves that she had trapped the latent genius into a loveless marriage. How she hated incestuous college gossip. As if it was any of their goddamn business.

'He loved me once too,' she wanted to scream at the top of their collective heads. 'And I loved him. I was the only one who did. When he was a nobody.'

And now, because he had become a somebody and in the process had fallen for somebody else, she was supposed to step quietly aside, not make a fuss, accept the inevitable. Disappear. Well, bad luck.

'Till death us do part, remember?' she'd said during some half-forgotten, half-recalled argument of not so long ago.

A wave of vertigo overtook her. She clutched at the rail, wishing she hadn't had the second surreptitious sherry... or the third. She wouldn't have had either if it hadn't been for the phone call. The phone calls were what unnerved her most. Bloody things. More and more frequent of late. Violating her security, eating away at her inner space, unravelling what was left of her self-esteem.

She had come to dread the hesitant silence at the end of the line, the sudden indrawn breath, as though the unseen caller was about to speak, to reveal all, to make her worst fears reality. And then the receiver replaced with a click, leaving her in a void with her unconfirmed doubts and a bottomless pit where her stomach used to be.

She was halfway down the wide oak staircase when the doorbell rang, shrilling all conversation to silence. Heads turned in anticipation as Gareth, handsome as the Devil, raffish in red tights, pranced to the door, tail swishing behind him.

Outside on the step, shrouded in the night mist, Olwyn's doppelganger stood framed in the doorway. A black-clad figure, complete with fright wig and conical hat, back-lit by the watery moon.

Gareth paled visibly under his pointed beard, brandishing his pitchfork at the apparition and stepping back a pace.

'Don't look so surprised, darling, it's only me,' and 'Meredith' shouted Lucifer in a tone of raucous relief, sweeping the stygian figure into a huge embrace while the rest of the room dissolved in laughter and applause.

Was there no end to the woman's infamy?

Meredith Hughes, the new college administrator, source of all Olwyn's angst, not content with seducing her husband, had also into the kitchen, straight to the cutlery drawer, extracting from it the biggest, sharpest knife in her collection. Enough was enough. She would put an end to this charade once and for all. And Devil take the hindmost.

Secreting the knife in the voluminous folds of her gown, she elbowed her way through the crowded salon and into the hall.

It was empty. The lovers had retreated to some more private place. The bedroom probably. HER bedroom. Insult to injury.

Olwyn panted up the stairs, heart racing, lips drawn back beneath her death-mask, thin body shaking in a St Vitus dance of righteous indignation, driven by a blood-lust made all the more powerful from having been kept too long contained. She slammed into the bedroom, arm raised like a striking snake.

But someone had got there before her.

Meredith Hughes lay face down on the dressing table counter in a pool of congealing blood.

The knife clattered from Olwyn's hand. A knife identical to the one that protruded from her nemesis' back. The same knife.

The scream, echoing round the house, rattled the rafters and brought a few brave souls scuttling to the scene of the crime. At the forefront, reflected in the mirror, a tall figure dressed in fustian. A witch.

'But which witch?' thought Olwyn, grasping at clarity through the encroaching fog.

Elbowing through the gawpers now came Gareth, horns awobble, feigning surprise. 'My God,' hoarsely. 'What's happened?'

'The windows are open,' said the witch. Meredith Hughes, re-incarnated, her very voice. 'She must have disturbed an intruder. What a dreadful thing.' But the eyes behind the mask sparkled, triumphant.

Olwyn tried to cry out then, to tell them of Gareth and the inblown leaves. But the flash of déjà vu prevented her. Her husband's face behind her in the mirror just before he turned to open the window, the sharp burst of pain in her back as the knife went in.

They turned the lifeless body over, husband and lover, stripping away the death mask.

Fishbelly skin. Bloodless lips.

Not a pretty sight.

'I look like death,' thought Olwyn, finally understanding why everyone had ignored her for the past half hour.

History: Another Me story, the title inspired by a funny song performed by comedienne Hermoine Gingold who, offered the part of one of the three crones in Macbeth *and loathe to commit herself until she's counted the lines, asks the casting director—"Which witch?" It was also included in* Cold Cuts 3, *the Alun Books anthology launched during the 1995 Year of Literature at the "Welcome to My Nightmare" weekend in Swansea, where co-incidentally, I was writer in residence.*

NOBODY THINKS HE'S A BAD GUY

H E WAS THE pain and the pain was him.
The pain of eyes gouged out with blunt knives, of baby heads smashed against walls, of women nailed to trees through amputated breasts.

His mother on her knees forced to pleasure a grinning monster while another took her from behind. Choking, weeping. Not human in their eyes. Treated like an animal. Worse than an animal.

They had tied him to a chair so he could watch her humiliation, screaming for them to stop, powerless to end her shame. He strained at the bonds that cut through the skin of his wrists, his heart pounding with the horror of it, his mind blurring, trying to blot it out.

Enough. Let her go. He would tell them anything.

His mother cast aside like a piece of garbage, blood pooling beneath her violated body, left with nothing but fear and nausea and memories that would forever haunt her until she blotted them out with a rusty knife drawn across her wrists, an empty bottle of meths beside her, unwashed, uncared for, in a rat infested alley in the bombed-out remains of the city.

He woke with a jolt, bathed in sweat, a band of light falling across his blood-shot eyes.

Outside, the sun shone down on a tranquil landscape. Through the bars of the narrow window which gave onto the exercise yard of the interrogation building, he could see mountain peaks bordering a fertile valley down the centre of which a wide river wound lazily through green fields. A view peaceful as the first day of a wakening world. Like Eden had been. Before the creator's favourite child, Lucifer, son of the morning, fell from grace and, charismatic in his beauty and guile, introduced mankind to its dark side.

101

And let pain out of its box.

The siesta was over.

But the pain remained.

He rose from his truckle bed and observed himself in the cracked mirror, slicking back his dark hair, the agony throbbing in his temples now, travelling in bursts down the back of his neck into his spine, alerting all the exposed nerve-ends clustered there.

Just over the rise, on the other side of the gun-blasted stand of pines, in the lea of the great oak that had stood sentinel since Napoleon had swept through the valley, in a quiet white house smelling of newly baked bread and furniture polish, he imagined his mother cooking dinner, singing quietly to herself so as not to wake Anna.

As she'd sung when he had been a child.

And he, waking, would make no sound, drinking in the pure, clear tones, taking comfort from the sweetness of her voice, trying to forget the throb of the belt bruises from the latest beating, that she had tried to prevent and, in failing, had taken the blows on herself.

To protect him.

Rising when the song was done, he would creep into the garden to pull the wings off flies. Transferring the pain to something more vulnerable.

As he'd grown older and the beatings had become more savage, his fury and impotence had escalated, bringing with it the dissection of mice and stoats, peaking in the hounding of children smaller than himself, robbed of their innocence in secret ceremonies of his own devising, sworn to silence by the fear of more excruciating initiations to come.

Pain - a hard taskmaster.

It gripped him like a vice, leaving him no peace.

He thought of Anna, who called him the gentlest of lovers—the child big within her—stroking his hair, telling him he was the most wonderful man in the world.

Sometimes, afterwards, he would rest his head against the mound of her stomach, feel the baby quicken, and the pain would ease. For a moment. But no more than a moment.

Wounds—gaping, serrated. Stomachs torn apart, bayonet ripped, guts spilling, slithering down to the knees, the hands grasping to stop them falling out, eyes popping, mouths agape in disbelief. Shattered kneecaps. Splintered bone protruding through charred and broken skin. Grown men calling for their mothers. To kiss it and make it better. Mothers lying in alleyways, drunken, broken.

Secrets. Memories.

Soon now they would come for him. He would need to be ready. He must be strong. Show no fear in the face of the pain.

If only this current pain would go away. It beat against the inside of his skull like the tongue of a great bell, clanging in his pulse, reverberating in his veins. Bringing tidings of the enemy at the gates. Warning of rape and pillage and looting. Of genocide and murder. Of excruciating, unthinkable, unstoppable horrors to come.

Normality so close. His mother sweeping the flagstone floor. Anna batheing her bloated body, the skin so soft, so vulnerable in the pale light of the drawn curtains. Nothing to save the child but that wall of flesh. And flesh so fragile, so rendable.

His blood chilled at the thought, goose-pimples rising against the terror of possibilities—of being unable to stave off the human degradation and the ongoing, inescapable pain.

Irony.

His mother so proud of him. A Captain in the army—like his father before him—keeping the forces of chaos at bay.

He would survive it. MUST survive it. For them.

And he could. Until the night, when reality retreated, and his defences were down. Then the pain really came into its own. Getting its OWN back.

At night there was no escape.

At night the pain would creep out of the darkness, chuckling obscenely, running and re-running looped memories of scenes he would rather forget. In glorious technicolour and stereophonic sound. Then he would wake weeping, unable to shut out the bitter smell of vomit and excrement. Or hold the demons at bay.

Except with something worse.

Pain's sweet revenge.

Somewhere in the dungeons, someone began to scream. A high-pitched animal wail of terror and disbelief. Pain did that to you. Took you by surprise. Left you without defence. Unless you got there first.

A great shudder ran through his body. He turned from the windows, pressing the nails into the soft flesh of his palms to calm himself.

Time to prepare.

Slowly, he slid on the uniform jacket that he had hung on the back of the chair before he had laid down to rest, buttoning it up to the neck, checking in the mirror for stray hairs on the khaki shoulders, peering for cracks in the facade of his handsome, ruined face.

There were none.

The eyes were dead, of course.

But otherwise he looked almost human.

He took a bottle from his desk drawer and swallowed a bitter mouthful of neat gin, the raw alcohol rushing to his stomach, lightening his head. Then he settled himself behind the desk and placed the military cap on his head, the shiny black brim shading the empty eyes. The soul fled from behind them. By the things he'd seen. By the things he'd done.

His mother - or somebody else's. He couldn't remember. Like the babies. Like the crucified women. Like the gouged eyes and the torn out tongues and the screaming and the blood.

Why did he do it?

He knew why.

Not for a cause. Not because he liked it. But because he needed it to survive. To keep his own pain at bay.

Only the pain could relieve the pain.

Briefly, he checked at the tools of his trade, arranged neatly on the iron rack. The electric probes, the bastinado, the flaying knife, the pliers for ripping out nails, tearing teeth from gums. He touched each piece of equipment lovingly and strange calm settled over him, a relief that soon it would be over, for now, at least. The pain transferred, to other nerve-endings, other flesh.

Outside in the corridor he could hear the mutterings of the guards, see through the frosted glass of the door the huddled shapes of today's suspects, their trousers already wet with the anticipation of what they could not avoid.

Their fate.

And his.

Placing his perfectly manicured hands palms down on the desk top, he took three deep breaths to calm the last vestiges of terror in his heart.

He was the pain and the pain was him.

But he was safe.

For the moment, at least.

'Bring in the first prisoner,' he barked.

History: This thoroughly unpleasant little tale, commissioned by Steve Jones and Dave Sutton for Dark Terrors 6, *was inspired by the war crimes trials after the fall of the generals in Argentina and at the end of hostilities in the Balkans. Some of the details that came out were truly horrific. The ingenuity, along with the banality of evil often beggars description. Someone once said that we all have it within us to be either a Mother Theresa or a Hitler? So what makes a person choose the Dark Side? 'Nobody thinks he's a bad guy'. Everybody can justify their behaviour with some sort of reason, however warped. Even Adolf believed he was a saviour. And remember he didn't stoke the furnaces. The final solution wasn't even his idea. All he did was rubber stamp it. Not that that's an excuse. But it is the up close, redhot poker wielding madness of the up-close torturer that boggles the mind. What fuels that kind of insanity? Fear? Revenge? De Sadic titillation? Or is it an ancient impulse, lurking in us all, that causes some children to strangle kittens? Just because they can.*

THE SELKIE'S CAP

DONAL CAME UP from the bay, shook himself like a dog and headed off in the direction of town. He crunched purposefully over the gravel, eyes flicking right and left, searching out a marker in the sand dunes that divided the beach from the patchwork fields beyond.

A hundred yards down he found what he was looking for, a hump of bladder wrack, dark as a beached whale, nestling beside a large piece of driftwood. The perfect hiding place. Taking off his cap, he tucked it into the belly of the mound. Then he set off again.

The early autumn breeze held the promise of a hard winter to come. It ruffled his short dark hair and made his eyes smart. Under his Fair Isle pullover, relic of a long drowned sailor, he shivered, half in cold, half in apprehension.

It was the first time he'd been out of his element alone and he wondered whether his relatives weren't right when they said he wasn't old enough for such a journey. But Gregor would not last the winter and his one wish was to see his wife again before he died. No one else in the family would even speak her name, let alone volunteer to look for her and so eventually, reluctantly, they'd let Donal go.

As he hit the high road, a dirt track bordered by dry stone walls and scrub grass, the weathercock on the distant steeple winked like a lighthouse in the setting sun. Lowering his head against the wind, he trudged on.

Over the brow of the first hill a boy sat astride a wooden stile, aimlessly throwing stones at a dandelion. He was younger than Donal by about three mainland years and had the emaciated look of the half-fed and frequently beaten.

He and Donal sized each other up.

'Where did you spring from?' the boy said.

Donal waved vaguely in the direction of the shore. 'I'm looking for my mammy,' he said. 'She's been gone a while and my da's not well and he thinks she might be being kept against her will.'

'Held for ransom, eh?' said the boy. 'Is she a princess, then?'

Donal shook his head.'

'I didn't think so,' the boy grinned. 'Not by the state of your jersey anyway. Would you like some tea?'

'No. I'll need to get on.'

'All the more for us then.' The boy pointed to the rough stone croft that clung like a limpet to the barren hillside. 'But if you change your mind, that's our house up there. I'll ask my mammy if she's heard of any kidnappings hereabouts. Don't hold your breath though.' And with a final wave, he raced off up the slope.

Donal waited until the boy had entered the croft and shut the door behind him. Only then did he follow in his tracks up the heather-covered drumlin to the pinpoint of light that was the cottage window.

Inside, a woman in a worn dress stood stirring a panful of porridge with a wooden spoon. The boy from the road was washing his hands in an old iron sink. Two other children, about three and five respectively, sat at a table, spoons at the ready. A baby, not yet walking, played in the hearth with a collie pup.

'I met a laddie in the lane,' the boy was saying. 'His mammy's been kidnapped. She's a princess.'

'Whist, Rory,' said the woman, wearily. 'You're worse than your da with your fairy stories.'

'It's the truth,' protested the boy. 'He said she'd been gone a good while and that she was being kept against her will. His da is on his last legs,' he added dramatically. 'And he's been sent to find her.'

The woman turned suddenly, almost upsetting the porridge. Donal, nose pressed to the pane, felt his heart lurch. It was his mother.

He had not hoped to find her so easily or so soon. Yet there she was, her hair somewhat faded with the passage of the years, but her face still beautiful enough to stop hearts. She turned her limpid brown eyes to the window and Donal raised an arm in greeting.

'What're you up to, you skulking devil?'

A rough hand grabbed him by the collar, lifting him off his feet and shaking him like a rat. The whiskey breath almost overpowered him as he struggled to extricate himself from the vice-like grip. But the man was three times his size and had the brute strength born of years of back breaking work done in all weathers.

He swung Donal towards him, hand raised to strike, then his face blanched as he took in the dark eyes and the small, pink ears set close to the head. His grip loosened momentarily and Donal, taking his chance, squirmed free and hared down the hillside as fast as his feet would carry him.

'Come back, you thieving throwback.' The harsh voice sliced through the darkness like a harpoon. But Donal was well away, leaping the dry-stone wall into the lane, legs pumping like pistons, all the way back to the beach.

Screeching to a halt at last by the bladder-wrack hummock, he crouched down, breath like fire in his lungs, and scrabbled beneath the soft, damp seaweed for his cap. It was still there. But when it became clear that the man was not following him, he tucked it away again and sat back on his heels.

What was his mother doing with such a man? Why didn't she come home?

He thought of his own father, gentle, protective, as different from that cruel bully as chalk was from cheese. Anger bubbled up inside him. Whatever the danger, he must confront his mother and demand an explanation. He owed Gregor that, at the very least.

Slowly he rose and, with a last longing look towards the safety of the sea began the long trudge back to the cottage.

Hugging the wall for safety, he climbed the hill at a crouch, moving from the shadow of one boulder to the next until he stood in the lee of the windowsill. There he waited, heart pounding, gathering his courage. Then slowly, slowly, he stood up and peeped inside.

The table had been cleared and the children put to bed in a curtained alcove. The man lay, mouth ajar, snoring on the rocker. He had the red hair and freckles of a native islander. His skin, once eggshell pale, was veined by whiskey and weather.

The woman sat by the fire, a half-knitted sock held loosely in her lap, staring vacantly into the dying embers of the turf. There was a cruel bruise on her right cheekbone that hadn't been there before. As Donal made to tap, she laid her work aside and, wiping her eyes with the back of her hand, tip-toed to the door and stepped out into the silence of the pale, Hebridean night.

Down below, the still sea glittered silver under a waning moon. Gathering her shawl around her shoulders, the woman eased the door shut behind her and walked a few paces down the hill. Then she tilted her face to the sky and gave a small, shrill bark.

Donal barked in reply then moving to his mother he wrapped his arms around her, burying his face in her apron. His eyes prickled with held back tears.

'Whist,' said his mother, stroking his sleek head. 'We dinna want the man to hear us.'

'Gregor's dying,' said Donal, fiercely. 'He needs you. You must come.'

'I cannot, sweetheart.'

'Why can you not? How can you stay with that monster? Why did you leave us?' And much to his chagrin, for he had not wept in years, he began to cry.

His mother continued to stroke and soothe. 'I never left you, bairn,' she said. 'There has not been a moment these last seven years that I have not thought about you both.'

'Then why?'

'I was young and foolish. And the man was handsome then. A wordsmith. A poet. We met on the beach and he charmed me with his fine verses and his tales of the dancing in the town. I only meant to look. But he had seen me hide the cap. He stole it. And though I have searched high and low, I have never been able to find it. And so I am trapped here. And there's nothing I can do.'

'I'll find it,' promised Donal. 'And then you'll come home.'

'Then I'll come home.'

'What about the other bairns?' Donal, suddenly contrite, remembered the desolation he had felt after his mother had gone.

'Someone will take them in,' said his mother, sadly. 'His mother is a good woman. She'll not see them starve. Wherever they go they'll be better off without him. Cruelty is all that he knows. But I doubt it'll come to that. The cap has vanished. I fear he has destroyed it.'

For a full week Donal stalked the red-headed soul stealer. Like an otter after a sea-trout, he slithered face down in the heather, lurking behind walls, following in the man's wake each day as he took the coracle out to the fishing grounds. During these expeditions he also managed to replenish his food store. But he dare not close his eyes for fear that his quarry might chose that time to return to the scene of the crime.

At night, while the island slept, he scoured the hillside, upturning every stone, exploring every cave and cranny. When that was done he searched the beach from end to end.

But of the cap, there was no sign.

Eventually, on the seventh day, dog tired and weary to the bone, he made his way into town, to the tavern, where the man and his cronies were swilling beer and singing raucous songs.

Shivering with cold, Donal kept vigil in the street outside, watching through the window, straining his ears for a word or sign that would lead him to the thing he sought.

Around dusk it began to rain. Not the sudden fresh downpour that sweeps the streets and clears the air, but that steady, bone-drenching drizzle that knows neither beginning nor end.

After an hour of it Donal, asleep on his feet, decided to take refuge in the large, grey church whose weather-cocked steeple had beckoned to him on his first day ashore. Finding it locked, he dodged into the building next door. There was lettering over the lintel that he could not decipher. Six runes in all, the first and the last identical, their shape rising like the twin peaks of a magic mountain.

Inside there were many wonderful things on display, and for the first time in several days he felt at home. Here was the skeleton of a shark, there the jawbone of a whale. There were shells and pebbles and round, gold coins, the sort that littered the seabed where the old Spanish treasure ship had sunk. There was a coracle too and a ship in a bottle. Donal was just wondering how they got such a large rig through such a small opening when a voice behind him nearly made him jump out of his skin.

'You're dripping all over my nice clean floor,' it said.

Donal turned to find a pleasant-looking woman in tweeds, grey hair pulled back in a bun, regarding him with an exasperated expression through horned-rimmed spectacles.

'You're not from hereabouts,' she said. 'What are you doing in the Museum?'

Donal flattened himself against the wall. 'It's raining,' he faltered.

'I can see that,' said the woman. 'You've brought most of it in with you. Where's your mother? Why aren't you at school?'

Donal shook his head, wordlessly.

'Well, you can't stay here. We're just about to close.'

The woman took a large umbrella out of a stand by the door and made to lock up.

'I want to go home.' Donal drooped with fatigue.

'Are you lost?'

Donal nodded.

'Poor boy.' The woman patted him on the head, drew back a saturated hand. 'Heavens, you're soaked. If you don't dry off soon, you'll catch your death. I'll tell you what. You wait here and I'll pop across and check at the bus station. Your mother's probably over there worried to death about you. While I'm gone you can have a look at out prize exhibit. It's what all the tourists want to see. It's over there in the corner.'

Donal dragged his unwilling feet across the room to the glass case resting on a fat plinth beneath an arched window. Inside, nestled on a bed of red velvet, lay a small, grey, conical object made of animal fur.

'It's a Selkie's cap,' said the woman, as if he didn't know. 'They say the seal people can change into humans at will. But if they lose the cap they can't get back. It's only a legend of course, but it makes a nice story, don't you think?'

'Where did you get it?' Donal tried not to sound too interested. The cap might be anyone's. Might be a hundred years old. Might not be his mother's at all.

'A man brought it in. A local. About seven years ago. Said he found it on the beach.'

That settled it.

Donal grimaced. Such cunning. Hiding it in plain view. Knowing his mother would never come inside such a thing as a Museum.

'Can I touch it?' he said, trying the lid, finding it locked.

'Certainly not.' The woman sounded scandalised. 'Don't touch anything at all. I'll be right back.'

And she darted off into the rain.

Donal looked around for something with which to prize open the lid, found nothing suitable. Finally, in desperation and knowing time was short, he lifted a large marble bust of some long-dead notable and smashed it through the glass. Then he grabbed the cap and fled.

He was half-way down the road when he heard the familiar voice, bellowing 'Stop thief.' Never halting in his stride, he looked over his shoulder. The woman was dancing up and down in the gathering dusk, gesticulating frantically to a man in a dark blue suit and a peaked cap who stood by her side. Curious onlookers were beginning to emerge from adjacent shop doorways to see what all the fuss was about. Then man in blue took something silver out of his pocket and blew on it. It emitted a high pitched wail that made Donal's hair stand on end.

And then the tavern door burst open and the red-headed man staggered out, swaying on drunken legs, crowded onto the pavement by a quartet of equally inebriated companions. A word from the woman and he was suddenly sober, lurching off down the cobblestones in hot pursuit.

Donal ran as he had never run before, the gathering mob howling after him. Past houses and shops, stores and garages he raced, till the dwellings dwindled and he was once more in open country.

Still the rain pelted down. He shut his eyes against its ferocity, running blind now, trusting to his animal instinct to keep him from stumbling, while behind him his pursuers bayed their blood-lust to the darkening sky.

Down the road he fled, fording the stone wall at a breach in the masonry where the fallen stones made a handy step-over. Cutting up and across country, he raced towards the solitary cottage, his mother's passport to freedom clutched in one sweating hand.

Bursting into the house, he grasped the startled woman by the arm, dragging her out and down the hill towards the safety of the sea. Behind her, the baby began to cry and she half-turned, like Lot's wife, to look back.

Then the crowd crested the hill, armed to the teeth with sticks, stones, broken bottles, anything they could lay their hands on along the way, heedless of who they were after or why. A lynch mob now, devoid of reason or humanity.

Donal climbed the style and his mother followed, catching her apron on a spur of wood, worrying it free, following him across the dunes along the beach to the driftwood marker and the second cap. For one heart-stopping moment, as he scrabbled away at the sea-wrack, Donal thought the man might have found it.

But it was still there.

When, moments later, the mob crested the dunes, blood up to batter and bruise, woman and child had disappeared.

The man with the red hair and the biggest stick scanned the horizon, his face bestial with fury and frustration. Finally, realisation dawned and, dropping to his knees, he howled his loss into the approaching storm.

'Moraaaaag.'

The guttural human cry echoed across the water, almost obscuring the thrumming of the rain. As if in answer, the sky threw back a bolt of lightning, electrifying the air and illuminating the coastline.

Out in the bay, two sleek grey heads bobbed side by side, swimming strongly for the open sea and sanctuary.

History: Mike Ashley commissioned 'The Selkie's Cap' for his Fantasy Tales *anthology, which was published by Robinson in 1996. A bumper book with 28 stories by authors old and new, it was popular enough to go into a second print run and Random House New York brought out the American version in 1997.*

THE KROTON'S REVENGE

DONNY WEBBER SLUMPED into the kitchen with his hands thrust deep into the pocket of his blue jeans and an expression of extreme disgust plastered on his freckled face. Behind him, tongue lolling in the midsummer heat, drooped his faithful mongrel and constant companion, Butch. The summer holidays were only half-way through, his best friend Irving was away visiting his grandma in Seattle and time was hanging very heavy on Donny's hands.

'Can I have a glass of orange juice, Mom?' he asked, heading for the nine-foot Frigidaire that stood humming in the corner.

'What another one?' asked his mother. 'That's the sixth this afternoon. You'll be looking like an orange soon.'

'Please, Mom,' Donny wheedled. 'It's so hot.'

'Well, all right,' agreed his mother, reluctantly. 'But this is the last one, mind. And then you and that mutt of yours can just clear out of my kitchen. I've got enough on my plate without having you two under my feet all day. Go play outside, why can't you?'

'There's nobody to play with,' complained Donny. 'Gee, Mom. I'm bored.'

'Bored?' exclaimed Mrs Webber. 'Why there must be a million and one things you could be doing on a lovely day like this.'

'Such as what?'

'Such as what about that radio-controlled aeroplane your father bought you for your birthday? It cost him a fortune and you haven't had it out more than twice since. Why don't you take it down and fly it in the park?'

'Hey.' Donny brightened up. 'That's not a bad idea. Come on, Butch,' and he bounded up the stairs, two at a time, to collect the aerodynamic wonder that had set Mr Webber back a third of his week's wages.

'Careful crossing the road,' called his mother, as Donny and Butch careered down the stairs again and out of the kitchen door.

'And don't be late for supper.'

Across town, at the headquarters of Mammoth Pictures Inc., a very important script conference was in progress. It involved three people. Sam Lastfogel, creator and writer of the 'Kroton' movies, Ed Levine, yes-man to the mighty and the President of MPI himself, that much feared movie mogul and master of all he surveyed, Cedric G. de Thrille.

The great man slid the king-sized cigar to one side of his king-sized mouth and gave forth.

'I don't like it, Sam,' he rasped. 'The script's all wrong. Am I right, Ed?'

'Right, C.G.'

'It's old hat. It doesn't have any pizzazz. It doesn't grab me. Does it grab you, Ed?'

'No, C.G. I can't say that it does.'

'See, Sam. It doesn't grab Ed either. And if it doesn't grab us then it ain't gonna grab the audience.'

'But I don't understand, C.G.,' said Sam Lastfogel, an edge of desperation in his voice. 'It was your brief. The script's exactly the way you wanted we should do it.'

'Well, I guess I changed my mind,' said the Studio Boss. 'Or maybe you're just losing your touch, Sam? I mean take the title. '*The Kroton's Revenge?*' Now what kind of a title is that? It's got no...' He clicked his fingers. 'What's the word I want?'

'Charisma, C.G.?' suggested Ed.

'Right. Charisma. It's got no charisma. And anyway, monster movies are dead in the water. Washed up. Kaput. Am I right Ed?'

'Always right, C.G.'

'Disaster movies. They're the big thing nowadays. They tell me the Weiner Brothers are working on one at the moment about the Empire State Building being struck by lightning in the middle of the rush hour. Now if you could come up with something like that...only bigger and better, naturally.'

'Naturally,' echoed Ed.

'But C.G.,' pleaded Sam. 'You can't just put the Kroton out to pasture. I mean, think of his fans. Think of him. How's he gonna take it?'

'Get real, Sam.' C.G.'s laughter grated like chalk against a blackboard. 'To hear you talk anyone would think the Kroton was real. When all's said and done, what is he? A hunk of metal and electronics covered in some mangy old fur.'

'But, what's to become of him?' Sam wanted to know.

'Well, we can't keep him on the lot, that's for sure. He takes up far too much space. And space is money. You agree Ed?'

'Oh, yes, C.G. Absolutely, C.G. Space is money indeed.'

'Soooo...There's only one thing for it...' The big chief paused to take a puff of his cigar.

'You don't mean...not...the scrap yard?' Sam was horrified.

Cedric G. de Thrille nodded sagely. The Kroton's fate had been sealed.

'But...but you can't,' stammered Sam. 'Think of all the money he's made for you. I mean the least you could do is put him in the Movie Museum.'

'Sorry, Sam.' The Big Boss shook his head, ruefully. 'The budget just won't run to it. The upkeep. You get the message? Besides, my mind's made up. We gotta move with the times.'

'Yes,' agreed Ed. 'Move with the times. How wise.'

'And what about me?' asked Sam.

'Well, Sam, it's like I said. If you can come up with an idea for a good disaster epic, we can talk turkey. If not...' He left the implication hanging in the air.

'You mean I'd be for the scrap yard too?' said Sam, bitterly.

'There'd be a financial settlement, of course,' said C.G, magnanimously. 'Never let it be said that I'm not a generous man.'

'Never let it be said,' said Ed, with a smirk.

This was the last straw. Suddenly Sam was furious. He looked from one unsympathetic face to the other, the one, hard as nails, the other knowing which side its bread was buttered on. Then he stood to his feet, rage dissolving his long-felt fear of the Studio Boss who paid his meagre wages.

'Keep your blood money, you ungrateful old coot,' he seethed.

'You know as well as I do that the Kroton made this Studio. For twenty years he's paid for your swimming pools and your Cadillacs and your Yes-Men.' He shot a look of pure vitriol at Ed Levine, who shuffled uncomfortably under his gaze. 'So now you're tired of him?' Sam went on. 'And what thanks does he get? None. A big fat zero. You want to throw him in the ash-can with the rest of your cast-offs. Well, that doesn't include me. I wouldn't soil my hands with your lousy pay-off, you bald headed old megalomaniac. You can shove it where the sun don't shine.'

Cedric G. de Thrille had gone a peculiar shade of puce. In all his years as the head of Mammoth Pictures, no-one had ever spoken to him in such a fashion.

And he didn't like it. He didn't like it one little bit.

'Get out of here, you low life,' he gargled, struggling to his feet. 'You're fired.'

'You're too late,' yelled Sam. 'You can't fire me. I just quit!' And he stomped out of the office, yanking the door shut viciously behind him.

Gloria Curvy, Mr de Thrille's blonde secretary, who happened to be painting her toe-nails at the time, looked up from her third little piggy in surprise. When the intercom went, she almost up-ended her bottle of varnish. Scarlet Starlet. The very latest shade.

'Yes, C.G.?' she squeaked.

'Call security.' C.G.'s stentorian tones crackled over the airwaves. 'If that bum isn't off the lot in five minutes, I'll know the reason why.'

But Sam was already on his way, storming through the outer office and into the corridor, which led to the series of small cubicles that constituted the writer's quarters at MPI. He slammed into the one with 'Sam Lastfogel' inscribed in gold lettering on the door.

In the two minutes that it took him to empty the contents of his desk into his battered briefcase, he had stopped feeling angry and started feeling sorry for himself. It didn't take a rocket scientist to realise that putting someone like C.G's nose out of joint would ensure that he 'never worked in this town again'. Taking a last look around the little room that had seen the birth of the Kroton twenty years before, he was near to tears.

Slowly, he walked down to the back lot where his creation was stored between pictures, to say a last 'goodbye'.

Beside the electronic control panel, which guided his movements, Sam Lastfogel's brainchild rested in a cage constructed from reinforced steel.

'The Kroton' stood ten meters high and measured two metres across his chest. His long, muscular arms, covered in sparse ginger fur, ended in massive, six clawed hands. The short stumps that supported his powerful frame tapered into horny webbed feet. His face, if you could call it that, had the flat, flare-nostrilled nose of a gorilla and a single beady eye that glinted with malice. But it was the mouth that was his most arresting feature. It was even bigger than C.G.'s and filled with a double row of serrated teeth, as pointed and perilous as those of a killer shark. In repose, his lips were drawn back in a fearsome snarl.

He was not exactly a pretty sight, but Sam Lastfogel loved him like a baby. He put a hand through the bars and patted one six-taloned claw gently.

'Goodbye, old fella,' he sniffed, wiping away a tear. 'And thanks...for everything.'

'Hey, Butch,' said Donny, manipulating the handset that controlled his birthday present. 'Just look at that thing go.'

Butch yawned an uninterested, canine yawn as the silver and blue machine dipped and swooped across the cloud-free stretch of summer sky. As far as he was concerned, this was an afternoon wasted. Parks were for romping in, for playing 'fetch', for general horsing around. He didn't see anything amusing about making a silly plane fly about.

'Wheeee,' yelled Donny, setting his new toy through a complicated series of victory rolls. 'Get a load of that style.'

He moved the appropriate lever and the plane banked before beginning a steep skyward climb. Up, up it went until it was just a tiny black speck in an ocean of blue.

'Watch this, Butch,' he shouted. 'I'm gonna make her do a nose-dive.'

Butch obediently lifted his damp muzzle from where it had been resting on his front paws and cast a desultory eye heaven-wards.

Donny twiddled another of the controls and the plane did a loop the loop and began to hurtle towards the ground.

'I'm not going to pull her out of it until she's almost into that tree,' he declared, as the silver streak continued its descent, gathering momentum the while. 'It's just a matter of not losing your nerve.'

At the very last minute before impact he made to move the lever.

But the lever was stuck.

Frantically he worried the controls with his sweat sticky hands. But it was no good. In a final, spectacular burst of speed the plane smashed, with a screech of tearing metal, into the branches of the tall Canadian Maple.

Donny hurled the control unit to the ground and raced across to the tree.

'Good golly,' he said, staring up in dismay to where the wreck hung, sadly entwined in the foliage, about ten feet in the air. 'Well, there's only one thing for it, I suppose!' and he began to shin up the trunk.

Butch hoisted himself up and slunk over to where the control unit lay nestling in the grass. Now was his chance. If he could take the thing away and hide it, perhaps Donny would spend the rest of the afternoon playing 'fetch'. The day wouldn't be a total write-off. Surreptitiously, he picked the unit up in his mouth.

'Hey!' shouted Donny, who was now straddled in a fork half way up the tree. 'Put that down, Butch, y'hear?'

Caught in the act, Butch snapped his mouth shut in surprise. As he did, one of his pointed incisors pierced the remote control panel, short circuiting a couple of wires and setting up a high pitched whine that penetrated his doggy skull with ferocious intensity. He shook his head to try to dislodge the unit but his tooth only became more embedded.

'Put that down, I said,' hollered Donny, almost losing his balance. From his vantage point in the tree he could see Butch shaking the control unit in apparent fury. The frequency at which the tone was being transmitted was much too high for a human ear to register, so naturally he didn't understand what was going on. To his amazement, Butch began to do a Samba round the tree trunk, shaking his head frantically in time with some imaginary rhythm section.

Donny abandoned his rescue plan and began to clamber down.

But Butch's was not the only ear to respond to the broken control unit. In a certain back-lot at MPI the sound had triggered the Kroton's controls. The finely tuned mechanism that operated Sam Lastfogel's beloved invention began to click and whirr into life.

Mamie 'The Mop' Johnson leaned on her broom in the same back-lot enjoying a quiet and strictly forbidden smoke. In between puffs she contemplated her afternoon's handiwork and began to carol an out-of-tune ditty.

'Some dayee he'll come along-ah. The man I love-ah.'

Behind her, the Kroton stirred. His gigantic head turned first to the left, then to the right. His pink tongue flickered out from between his yellow stained teeth.

'And he'll be big and strrrrong-ah. The man I love-ah,' warbled Mamie, blissfully oblivious to the fact that only three feet from her ample rear, a six taloned hand was reaching forward to grasp the reputedly unbendable, steel bars.

'And when he comes my way, ah,' sang Mamie, grinding the cigarette butt into the floor with a downtrodden heel, 'I'll do my best to make him stayeeeee...'

A rumbling roar interrupted her in mid screech. Tentatively she peered over her shoulder. What she saw made her eyes pop out. The Kroton had succeeded in bending the unbendable and was in the process of clambering out of his cage.

Mamie cast mop, bucket and other accoutrements to the four

winds. She was already screaming her news to an incredulous world by the time the Kroton's webbed feet had paddled through the spilt cleaning fluid and reached the outer door.

Come here you stupid mutt,' shouted Donny, desperately.

He had been chasing Butch for at least fifteen minutes but somehow the dog managed to keep one jump ahead of him. How he did it while stopping every three or four paces to roll over and paw at his mouth, was more than Donny could fathom.

Poor Butch was half deafened and to add insult to injury, his cavortings only served to impale the defective control unit even more securely in place. He bounded and wriggled around the park, turning amazing canine cartwheels, but still the unbearable, piercing din shrilled in his head.

A very puffed Donny scrambled after him, entreating, cajoling, threatening, pleading, begging him to stand still.

But Butch bounced unheedingly on.

The Kroton had demolished three cameras, two lighting consoles and the entire saloon set for 'Gunfight on the Santa Fe Trail, not to mention the electric circuit box that normally worked him and with which somebody could have turned him off, before he eventually reached the corridor leading to C.G.'s office. The entire studio was in a state of disarray. The employees of Mammoth Pictures Inc, from directors to tea boys, fleeing the path of the marauding monster in blind panic, did almost as much damage as the Kroton himself.

A snivelling Ed Levine rounded on his boss in a manner that was heretofore unthought of.

'It's all your fault, you big bully,' he gibbered. 'If you hadn't blabbed your big mouth off about sending him to the scrap yard none of this would ever have happened.' He shuddered, quaking in his correspondent shoes before diving under his desk. His voice rose in a sepulchral whisper from his hiding place. 'It's just like that script you rejected. The Kroton is coming to take his revenge.'

As if on cue the monster burst through the door of the outer office. Miss Gloria Curvy, cowering behind her typewriter, rolled her baby blue eyes heavenwards, emitted a shriek that would have done Fay Wray proud, and fainted dead away.

Meanwhile, back in the park, Donny had elicited the aid of the Park Keeper in a last ditch attempt to catch the culprit. Butch's acrobatics had become ever more extreme and the three of them scurried back and forth among the trees like a trio of demented circus performers. They were beginning to draw a crowd.

'Seems to me like he's gone plumb crazy,' panted the Park Keeper, as Butch executed a particularly deft back flip, one which drew a smattering of applause from the assorted onlookers.

'I can't understand it,' said Donny. 'He's never like this, normally.'

'Tell you what,' said the Keeper, who was starting to feel like it might be time for him to take early retirement. 'Let's you and me try to head him off at the pass. If we can herd him into that corner over by the wire, maybe then one of us'll get a chance to jump him?'

Backed into yet another corner, namely that of his sumptuous office, Cedric G. de Thrille was trying to parlay his way out of the trickiest situation of his life.

'Now listen, old fella, old friend,' he was saying, in a feeble attempt at chumminess. 'You didn't believe all those things I said before, did you? All that stuff about the scrap yard? Just my little joke. Heh Heh.' He gave a sickly grin. 'You know I wouldn't do a thing like that to you, old buddy, old pal. Why, where would Mammoth Pictures be without the Kroton?'

With a roar, the monster grasped C.G.'s quivering body in its scaly claws and lifted him towards the huge, tooth filled cavern that was its mouth.

'Argggh...' The studio chief shrieked, his pallid jowls dancing up and down in terror. 'No...No...Put me down. Put me down. I didn't mean it. Please, Mr Kroton, Your Majesty, Sir. I'll do anything you want. Anything. We'll make the movie. We'll make half a dozen movies. I promise on my honour. Just let me go.'

But the Kroton was oblivious to C.G.'s supplications. His hairy arms lifted his victim higher and higher, pulling him closer and closer to his cavernous maw.

C.G began to blub. Tears sprang from his mean little eyes and trickled down to drip off his bulbous nose.

'Save me, somebody,' he howled. 'Save me. *HELLLLLP.*'

At precisely this moment, in a piece of inspired timing that couldn't have been bettered by the dream factory itself, two things happened simultaneously. Sam Lastfogel walked into the head honcho's office with his hands in his pockets and, down in the boondocks, Donny finally managed to collar his errant pet.

'Gotcha,' Donny shouted, triumphantly, as he and the Park Keeper landed simultaneously on the struggling Butch. 'Now give that here.'

He prized the piece of battered machinery out of the squirming dog's mouth. As he dislodged it, the wires causing the short circuit came apart, the noise in Butch's head stopped and the remains of the plane fell out of the Maple tree.

Abruptly, the electronics powering the Kroton, juddered to a halt.

Half an inch away from those japing jaws, C.G. heaved a heartfelt sigh of relief and looked down at his erstwhile script writer who, unsure of how all this had happened, still wasn't a man to let such a heaven sent opportunity go by the board.

'OK, Sam,' C.G. rasped. 'You win. *The Kroton's Revenge*' goes into production next week.'

'Unlimited budget?' asked Sam, narrowing his eyes.

C.G. winced.

Furtively, Sam nudged the Kroton with his toe. The monster's superstructure shuddered, threateningly.

'OK. OK.' stammered C.G. 'Unlimited budget.'

'And if and when the big fella retires, the Kroton has pride of place in the Movie Museum?'

For a moment C.G. looked as though he was going to object. There were limits after all, and he *was* Head of the Studio. But again, the Kroton began to shudder and a threatening growl emanated from the drawn back lips. Sam Lastfogel looked startled. This time he hadn't done anything at all. But whatever, the growl had the desired effect.

'Yes, yes, yes,' said C.G. through gritted teeth. 'Unlimited budget and pride of place in the Movie Museum. You got that Ed?'

'Got it C.G.,' said Ed, crawling out from under the desk.

'Oh, and Ed.'

'Yes, C.G.?'

'YOU'RE FIRED.'

'Donny Webber,' scolded his mother, as a dirt encrusted Donny mooched into the kitchen with a bedraggled Butch trailing behind. 'Where have you been? I told you not to be late for supper. It's gone six already. And look at the state you're in.'

She eyed the battered remains of Donny's birthday present in horror.

'What in the world have you done with your aeroplane? Why it's ruined. If I were you I'd get that in the trash can and out of sight before your father gets home. I don't know,' she continued, shaking her head. 'Kids nowadays got no respect for property. You must think we're made of money. It doesn't grow on trees, you know?'

'Gee, Mom,' said Donny. 'It was a tree that was the problem. I couldn't help it. The controls jammed and the plane crashed into that big Maple and I was just trying to get it down and then Butch got hold of the console and he had some kind of a fit and...'

'And I'll have some kind of a fit if you don't get out of those filthy clothes and into a hot bath this instant. And then straight to bed with no supper, young man. Coming home at all hours. As for that dog, it's the outhouse for him.'

'Yes, Mom,' said a defeated Donny, heading for the stairs while Butch tried to slink under the couch.

Mrs Webber felt a twinge of remorse as she watched her son's retreating back. Had she been too hard on him? Boys would be boys and he was on his holidays after all. As he reached the bend in the stair she moved across and called up through the banisters

'Oh Donny.'

'Yes, Mom?'

'Come on down when you've gotten into your PJ's and we'll say no more about it. I'll fix you some milk and cookies and you can watch the Monster Movie on TV before you go to bed.'

'Gee, thanks, Mom,' grinned Donny. 'What's on?'

'The Kroton, I think.'

'Oh, great,' yelled Donny, disappearing into the bathroom at a rate of knots. 'I'll be right down. I don't want to miss anything. The Kroton's my favourite.'

History: To me the Kroton was a cross between King Kong and the Kraken. When Ronald Chetwynd-Hayes commissioned a story from me for the 4th Armada Monster Book, my 'Lightbringer' Trilogy was being touted around Hollywood by publicist Quinn Donoghue, who later went on to produce The Gingerbread House. *Unfortunately my sword and sorcery epic was a bit ahead of its time. The special effects industry was nowhere near developed enough to deal with the elaborate products of my imagination. They didn't know what to do with it and the project eventually sank without trace. But not before the great Ray Harryhausen had been commandeered to do the monsters, should we ever get the thing off the ground. He and Quinn had worked together on* Sinbad *and it was a joy to meet the man at his home, however briefly and see some of his wonderful models in the flesh, as it were. From this inspiration sprang my Kroton. But of course rather than the great big monster of my story, Ray's equivalent would have been only about a foot high. Small, but perfectly formed as were all his masterpieces.*

THE LILAC TREE

WHEN THE BROCHURE dropped on the mat of her negative equity maisonette, Amanda had reached a crisis point in her life. At thirty-two, having spent the last ten years working harder than anyone else at the Press Agency, she'd just been gazumped in the promotion stakes by the Boss's unqualified nephew. Add to that the fact that her fiancé had recently absconded with her best friend's sister and there was no escaping that she had come to a dead end, not only in her chosen profession but also in her love life.

'This large country mansion,' read the blurb, 'founded as a retreat by the Knights Templar in 1226 and latterly home of the Clan Alexander, overlooks a wooded valley plentifully populated with wildlife. The private loch is liberally stocked with brown trout supplied by a mountain stream, which flows into it directly from the Scottish Highlands. A haven of seclusion from the stresses and strains of modern life.'

The place sounded perfect.

'Too perfect,' thought Amanda, who had written enough press releases in her life to know how far they could stray from the truth.

She set the handout aside and opened the only other piece of mail awaiting her attention. It informed her that her number, which she hadn't bothered to check, had come upon in the national lottery and asked whether she could keep next Friday week free since this was the day designated for a well known celebrity to present her with a cheque for half a million pounds.

Amanda looked out at the interminable London traffic grumbling past her rain-lashed window. Then she picked up the phone and told the Boss's nephew where he could stuff his job.

Two weeks later having deposited the remains of her winnings in the highest interest account she could find, Laura, clad from head to toe in St Laurent, booked herself first class onto the night train north for a mini break to Bonnie Scotland. Except for the slightly sozzled oil executive who tried to pick her up in the dining car, the trip was uneventful. She retired to her couchette with a good book and a miniature whisky and soda and encouraged by the soporific swaying of the coaches, was soon fast asleep.

Disembarking onto the cobbled forecourt of Aberdeen station was like taking a step back in time. A world away from the rush hour crush of the Northern Line. Fresh air, friendly faces and streets so clean you could eat your breakfast off them.

The man from Mercedes was waiting for her with the car she had ordered and, formalities completed, she took possession of her new toy and headed for the Highlands. Fifteen minutes easy driving across town brought her to a quiet road that meandered along Royal Deeside. An occasional rabbit skuttered out of the undergrowth and once, just before she stopped for lunch at a small wayside eating-house, a huge antlered stag raised its head from the river's edge where it had stopped to drink, to fix her with liquid brown eyes, before resuming his elegant loping progress up the glen.

By the time she reached Templar House Amanda was feeling more relaxed than she had done in years. The great granite structure, part castle, part country mansion, rose phoenix-like from its stand of surrounding trees. There was an air of permanence and tranquillity about the place - as though the world, with all its petty squabbles had passed it by.

And the man who greeted her, in kilt and well-worn Arran sweater, seemed almost as impressive as the house itself. Tall as a Viking, with dark hair curling at the back of his neck like a latter day Byron, he leant down to open the car door and took her hand in a firm grip, fixing her with unsettling grey eyes that were curious without being familiar.

'You will be Miss Leigh,' he said, a hint of a highland accent colouring his voice, and when Amanda agreed that she was the very same, he introduced himself as Robert Alexander, Laird of the Templar Estate.

'Please to call me Alex though,' he said, favouring her with a Sean Connery smile. 'All my friends do.'

Amanda smiled back frostily, determined not to be so easily charmed, while her host unloaded her bags and led her through the huge double doors, across a vast entrance hall tiled in black and white and up a wide staircase flanked by family portraits, to the suite of rooms that had been prepared for her. Ivory silk wall-paper, a carved oak ceiling, two vast windows hung with gold vel-vet drapes and a four poster bed, no less, damasked in clotted cream.

'I've put you in the Queen's chamber', said Alex. 'I hope it suits. It has the best view of the loch, right enough.'

'Don't tell me Queen Victoria slept here too?' Amanda said, cynically.

'Nothing so contemporary, I'm afraid' the Laird grinned. 'Mary, Queen of Scots is the Lady I'm meaning. She stayed here with Bos-well before they were married. They say you could hear the sound of their passion from one end of the estate to the other.' He glanced sideways at her and Amanda found herself blushing like a schoolgirl. 'That bed has seen some action in its time,' he went on, turning the knife in the wound. 'The third Marchioness is sup-posed to have entertained a Demon Lover in it. But don't be alarmed. We've changed the sheets since then.'

He crossed to the windows and flung one wide to let in the late afternoon sun.

'Came to her in the form of an eagle so the legend goes. She used to wait for him at this very window. Husband had her burned alive. Married the housekeeper who had denounced her. Both of them died of the plague. Make yourself at home,' he added gen-ially. 'If you're not too hashed I'll be back in twenty minutes to give you the guided tour.' And with a swish of the kilt and a slam of the door, he was gone.

The view across the lake was truly spectacular. Amanda was impressed in spite of herself. Bluebells carpeted the grass under the rhododendron bushes and a great wedge of golden daffodils spilled over from the lake's edge into the shallows. Hard by the dilapidated landing stage, which ran down from the boathouse, stood a lone lilac tree, its white blossoms reflected in the still water.

She was still sitting there, elbows on the sill, eyes peeled for amorous eagles, when Alex came back. She started as he put his hand on her shoulder for she hadn't heard the door open. One minute he wasn't there, the next minute he was. She glanced round at the strong, brown hand and was appalled at her sudden almost uncontrollable urge to rub her cheek against it. She blushed again, as if her host could read her mind. But if he could, he gave no sign of it. He simply shifted his grasp to her elbow and steered her out of the room.

It was clear that the man loved his home. At first she thought his enthusiasm might be a pose, but as he talked, guiding her over the old house, emphasising every feature, filling her in on its history, entertaining her with stories of his ancestors, scurrilous and honourable alike, she realised that there was no deception in him. He was what he seemed to be, a real, dyed in the wool, honest-to-god gentleman. She thought of the Boss's nephew, reflecting ruefully that such paragons were woefully thin on the ground these days.

Afterwards they strolled through the gardens reaching the ruined landing stage just as dusk was falling. The sky, shot through with bright blue and crimson, deepened into indigo as, side by side, they watched the moon rise over the distant mountains through the branches of the lilac tree.

That night they dined on fresh salmon and game pie. It was the staff's night off, Alex explained, and since she was the only houseguest, he would serve her himself. The polished oak table had been set with crystal glasses and the family silver, each piece marked with a coat of arms and the family motto 'Love and duty' in Latin. A fire burned in the huge stone grate 'to take the chill off the place' and Alex had changed into dress tartan 'in honour of the occasion'.

In his short black jacket, silver buttons gleaming in the candlelight, white lace ruffles spilling from throat and cuff, he looked like a throwback to the time of Bonnie Prince Charlie. Every inch the romantic hero. Very fanciable knees. Amanda found herself wondering whether what they said was true, that a real Scotsman never wore anything under the kilt.

'I can't believe this place isn't bursting at the seams,' she said, to take her mind off the thought. 'What you need is a good press agent.'

'Like you, you mean?'

'How did you know I was a press agent?' Amanda asked, startled.

'Oh, I have my spies,' Alex grinned. 'You wouldn't consider taking it on, I suppose?' he added, hopefully. 'With your experience and contacts you could open the place up. A house this size needs people in it. Otherwise it just turns into a shell.'

'I'm retired,' said Amanda, but if you could find somebody else, this is what I'd recommend,' and she launched into the spirit of 'the game' theoretically transforming Templar House into an exclusive Health Spa, offering sanctuary to the jet-lagged jet-set at outrageous expense.

'It shouldn't even cost that much to kit out,' she concluded. 'Bathrooms en suite, a couple of treatment rooms for massage and such, maybe a Jacuzzi, central heating certainly for the winter season. With the right business plan you could raise the capital from investors and make your money back in no time – with interest.'

'You make it sound so easy,' said Alex. 'I'm afraid I don't have much of a head for business.'

Amanda laughed, tongue loosened by the good bottle of claret. 'Ideally what you want, of course, is a resident ghost. A ghost with libido. Like Boswell. That would *really* sell the place.'

Alex reached across the table to cover her hand with his own. The warmth of his touch shot up her arm like molten fire. His eyes, dark as pewter, held her immobilised.

'You could save Templar House from a fate worse than death, you know,' he said, 'if you really wanted to. It's just mouldering away here. Like old bones.'

Amanda felt frozen in time, timeless, as though this suggestion was the most normal thing in the world, the one thing she'd been waiting for all her life. Alex rose from his place, moved round the table and held out his hand. And without a second's hesitation, Amanda took it.

She woke to the sound of the doorbell ringing. Warm sunlight, filtering through the open window, fell across the huge bowl of lilac blossoms someone had left on her bedside table. There was no sign of the Master of the House and for a moment she thought she had dreamt it all.

The ringing became more insistent and since nobody seemed to be about to answer it, she got out of bed and shrugged into the Janet Reger silk kimono.

Outside the window she spotted Alex, dressed in well-worn tweeds and standing with his back to her under the lilac tree gazing out over the loch. She tapped on the window to attract his attention but he didn't respond and so, assuming that the servants were all occupied with other things, she trotted downstairs to get the door.

The middle-aged man who stood at the top of the steps announced himself as Dougal McClintock of McClintock, Esslemont and Cameron, Solicitors and Property Conveyers.

'Might I come in, Miss Leigh?' he enquired politely. 'I'm sorry to confront you in your desabelles but I've a bittie business to discuss and I'd rather not do it on the doorstep.'

Amanda stood aside to let him enter and McClintock strode purposefully into the entrance hall, coming to a halt directly beneath the portrait of Alex which had pride of place at the bottom of the stairs.

'Would you like to get changed?' he asked and when Amanda said not to worry, she felt she was decent enough, the solicitor nodded delving deep into the pocket of his Crombie overcoat to produce a buff coloured envelope.

'You'll be pleased to know,' he said. 'That the owner has accepted your offer. He's glad to get shot of the place to tell you the truth, says it's a millstone round his neck, him being almost permanently in Australia.'

The pewter dark eyes observed Amanda sardonically over the solicitor's shoulder.

'Australia?' she said, and then, pulling herself together. 'What offer?

'For the house, of course,' said McClintock. 'You are Miss Amanda Leigh of Hampstead Garden Suburb, London, are you not?'

Amanda opened the envelope with hands that had developed a slight shake. Inside, the letter, typed on her own personal notepaper, stated briefly that, having recently come into some money and leased her London apartment to a Japanese businessman, she was now in a position to offer £250,000 for Templar House, its grounds and contents. It was signed in her own hand

She suddenly felt strangely light-headed, as though she was viewing the world from under water. 'But... but... I didn't write this,' she stammered.

'Then who did, pray?' McClintock's tone was that of a man who feels he is having his valuable time wasted.

Amanda looked up into the eyes in the portrait, grey and unfathomable as the loch and frantically tried to remember every detail of the previous night. Had she drunk more than was good for her, signed something she shouldn't have? All she could recall was the feel of his hands on her skin and his promise, made in the heat of the moment no doubt, that he would never leave her, always be there.

The solicitor followed her gaze, turning to observe the portrait in its heavy, gilt frame.

'Ah, Alex,' he said, affectionately. 'You should have seen this place when he lived here. Dinner parties. Dances. Hordes of folk up from Edinburgh nearly every weekend. Pity he never married. Always said he was waiting for the right girl to come along. Too late now.'

'Why? Don't they have girls in Australia,' said Amanda, furious that she'd been taken for a ride in more ways than one.

The solicitor looked at her strangely.

'Och, it's not him that lives in Australia,' he retorted. 'It's the cousin. Never even been to see the place. Couldn't care less. Not like Alex. Even after the accident they couldn't part him from it.'

Amanda's skin went cold. 'Accident?' she said.

'Did you not know?' McClintock said... and then. 'But indeed, who would have told you? Alex drowned in the loch ten years ago. He's buried under the lilac tree.'

History. I read a story once. I can't remember where I saw it of who it was by, but it was a love story about a young couple, the husband of which came back for an unexpected furlough from the trenches of the First World War. They spent an idyllic weekend together. But after the girl had seen him off at the station and returned home, it was to find the telegram on the mat saying he'd been killed the week previous. The story had a profound effect on me. Rather than being frightened by such a notion, I found it very comforting. Love triumphing over the Grim Reaper. So when June Smith-Sheppard came through asking for yet another one of my stories for the 'Me' magazine, this modern variation on an ancient theme almost wrote itself. Mind you, the fact that I'd just had a long Sunday lunch at one of the big Country House Hotels on the outskirts of Aberdeen, might have helped somewhat.

ABOUT SAMANTHA LEE

Samantha Lee was born in Londonderry and studied at Newry Grammar School and London's Central School of Speech and Drama. After fifteen years treading the boards, she took the quantum leap from one precarious profession to another, making the crossover via magazine articles and short stories to her first full length work – 'The Quest for the Sword of Infinity', volume one of the Lightbringer Trilogy, a Sword and Sorcery epic that unfortunately pre-dated computer game simulations. Her latest offering is yet another trilogy – the 'Demon' series, written for Scholastic's Point Horror imprint and now available as ebooks. In between she has covered just about every other aspect of the writing game, from dark fantasy to exercise and self-development books, via BBC plays, radio talks, movie screenplays, poetry, literary criticism and children's TV series. It amuses her that despite the rest of her considerable output, the thing she is most recognised for is having at one time scripted Thames TV's 'Rainbow'. None of the enclosed stories however, are suitable for 'littlies'.

Also available from Shadow Publishing

Phantoms of Venice
Selected by David A. Sutton
ISBN 0-9539032-1-4

The Satyr's Head: Tales of Terror
Selected by David A. Sutton
ISBN 978-0-9539032-3-8

The Female of the Species And Other Terror Tales
By Richard Davis
ISBN 978-0-9539032-4-5

Frightfully Cosy And Mild Stories For Nervous Types
By Johnny Mains
ISBN 978-0-9539032-5-2

Horror! Under the Tombstone: Stories from the Deathly
Realm
Selected by David A. Sutton
ISBN 978-0-9539032-6-9

The Whispering Horror
By Eddy C. Bertin
ISBN: 978-0-9539032-7-6

The Lurkers in the Abyss and Other Tales of Terror
By David A. Riley
ISBN: 978-0-9539032-9-0

Worse Things Than Spiders and Other Stories
By Samantha Lee
ISBN: 978-0-9539032-8-3

Tales of the Grotesque: A Collection of Uneasy Tales
By L. A. Lewis
ISBN: 978-0-9572962-0-6

Horror on the High Seas
Selected by David A. Sutton
ISBN 978-0-9572962-1-3

Creeping Crawlers
Edited by Allen Ashley
ISBN 978-0-9572962-2-0

Haunts of Horror
Edited by David A. Sutton
ISBN 978-0-9572962-3-7

Death After Death
By Edmund Glasby
ISBN 978-0-9572962-4-4

www.ingramcontent.com/pod-product-compliance
Lightning Source LLC
Chambersburg PA
CBHW050822180626
46814CB00004B/1414